SUBS DELIVERANCE

First Edition

Published by The Nazca Plains Corporation
Las Vegas, Nevada
2009

ISBN: 978-1-935509-08-0

Published by

The Nazca Plains Corporation ®
4640 Paradise Rd, Suite 141
Las Vegas NV 89109-8000

PUBLISHER'S NOTE
Subs Deliverance is a work of fiction created wholly by Anthony Thomas' imagination. All characters are fictional and any resemblance to any persons living or deceased is purely by accident. No portion of this book reflects any real person or events.

Cover Photo, FleshBlack, www.fleshblack.be
Art Director, Blake Stephens

– DEDICATION –

To boys everywhere, may they find someone to help them fly.

– DISCLAIMER –

SUBS DELIVERANCE

First Edition

Anthony Thomas

– CONTENTS –

The story of a boy very much into heavy, dirty, use and abuse, but only as a part-time occupation. Always searching for another high he finds himself in what could be a dangerous situation only to be rescued by one of his tormenters and carried off, happily, to a life of service.

This is another story of a boy seeking heavy use who, like his author, could not submit 24/7. He is aware that occasionally such use will enable him to fly but never quite attains real fulfilment.

I've only been lucky enough on a few occasions to enter that state of mind through pain and use where you want to laugh and cry with joy while writhing with pain, that merely being an adjunct to your condition.

Out of the blue, while being thoroughly misused, our boy meets Karl, a supposedly heterosexual young man just seeking a quick release on a Saturday night. The Gods have different ideas and over the next couple of weeks they connect on the physical, emotional and mental plains and finally settle to, one hopes, a long life together but more as partners rather than full master and slave.

This is a story I became very attached to. Originally it was planned to end after boy's abuse in the woods. Karl walked out of the shadows from the trees and took over. Somehow he managed to dispose of the other characters and make himself the other major player, in fact, when he finally faced his sub-conscious I consider him the stronger personality.

How I wish the author would have met someone like Karl. He certainly could make boy fly.

MASTER 173

ABOUT THE AUTHOR 179

– BIGSARGE –

CHAPTER ONE

I just loved nights like this, warm and sultry, no work the following day to get up for, feeling on top of the world, fit and randy with just enough alcohol to take the fetters off. As I rode my bike a couple of towns away to my intended rest stop I reveled in the feel of the wind over my legs and up my denim cut-off shorts almost to the crutch, also flowing over my chest through the half done zip on my jacket. Feeling the weight of heavy chain around my neck balanced by the leather straps round my cock and balls just waiting to be joined by the wrist and ankle restraints kept my mind and my cock well occupied for the hour it took me to cover the odd 60 miles.

When I pulled of the road into the dirty sandy parking area I could see my luck was probably in. There were three arctic lorries probably parked up for the night and several cars came into immediate view under the moonlight as I switched off my engine and heads, coasting over to the trees by the rest room to park up myself. I knew my body was slightly on display in the shadows as I removed my jacket and old boots, placing them in a pannier and taking out the leather restraints. Taking my time to fit them, ankles, wrists, upper arm, I made sure anyone watching got glimpses of various parts of my body being twisted and flexed in order to fit the straps. Finally passing another leather belt around my waist I stood up and moved slowly toward the restroom.

I knew there were eyes on my body as it moved in and out of the shadows and heard at least a couple of vehicle doors open and close during my journey. As I got closer it could be seen the lights were out, or more probably broken but that was no matter as I knew sufficient light came through the dirty skylights to see what might be happening without being bright enough to see any faults with the bodies that I anticipated making use of mine shortly.

It was the smell that always did it that mixture of damp cement mixed with piss and sex and the minute I walked through the door my erection hardened to an extent that was excitingly painful. It would have been hurting even if my cock and balls had not been strapped up the erection was so strong. As it was the sudden increase in constriction had me gasp and come to a stop and it took my eyes a moment to acclimatize and for my body to notice the floor was wet and slightly muddy from the evening showers under my bare feet, or that there were already a few men standing at the urinal.

I can't claim I was the best-looking guy in there but knew I looked good, especially dressed as I was. I felt myself to be on display and of course that was the general idea, it fucked with my brain to know other men were looking at my near naked body with only one thing on their minds. Sex. Hopefully some of them would be happy to use my body to get their rocks off. I'm 24, nearly six foot with a slim, reasonable body and mousy blond hair, no body hair as what little I do have is shaved each weekend. Making my way toward the urinal which consisted of a wide flush trough a couple of the present occupants moved to one side as I turned round and crouched down with my back to the cool piss soaked tiles.

It only took a moment before there was a short fat cock being waved around in front of my face, 'You want my piss boy?'

'Yes Please Sir.'

As you can see I was brought up to be polite. He wasn't the only one as within a moment there were two streams of piss playing over my face, body and open mouth, soaking my hair and running down to re-soak my shorts that hadn't been washed now for several visits to sites I'd discovered like this one.

'That's a real pig boy we got here.' 'Yeah! Seen him before. He's real good.' 'That's filthy.'

I didn't hear whomever that was leaving in a hurry.

'He'll be filthier before we leave.'

All that sort of talk was getting to me, helping to separate my mind from my body, allowing it to observe in wonder and enjoyment when my body got abused. It would take a while yet and a fair bit of action but I had the feeling something good was going to happen tonight.

'Get up!'

A hand slapped my face lightly and then yanking on my hair half pulled me erect.

'Drop those shorts boy. You won't be needing them for a while.'

All I had to do was unfasten my belt and wriggle my hips for the weight of the soaking shorts to pull them down to my ankles into the piss filled trough.

'Step right out of them now, they can stay down there and get nice and dirty for you to ride home in.'

I didn't recognize either the black face or the voice but either he'd been here and seen me used before or was a natural.

'Yes Sir!'

'You won't be needing this either but I will,' as he reached forward and removed the spare leather belt still lying loosely round my waist. 'I will need it won't I boy?' When I took a moment to reply his hand came up and backslapped my face left and right, 'Answer me.'

'Of course you will Sir. It's for there for your enjoyment.'

'That's better boy. Stand out here where everyone can see you better. You got any weights for those balls?'

'Yes Sir! In my shorts.'

'Don't fuck me around then. Get down there and fish them out.'

As I knelt to feel for my shorts laying in the half flooded trough it was my belt landed across my backside with a crack.

'Get a move on boy!'

It landed again, this time with enough force to jerk my body forward where my lowered head came in contact with the trough and I surfaced gasping and spluttering from being half drowned with a mixture of piss and whatever else had been falling in the trough that evening.

'Can't get enough eh? Have to see if we can give you the rest later on. The stalls stink enough to be full.'

Oh No! That was seldom my scene. This night may be going too far. Even so, I stood up, holding a couple of weights hanging on short chains in one hand and a pair of nipple clamps in the other which I held out toward him only to receive another couple of backhanders that half stunned me for a moment.

'I don't want them you stupid boy. They're for you. Put the clamps on, quick now.'

I couldn't help it but moan as I clamped them on my nipples and adjusted the side screws to increase the tension. My nipples had not been touched for several days and were not really ready for this sort of abuse, even so I gloried in the pain they induced.

'Hurts I hope?' he asked.

'Yes thank you Sir,' I replied.

'Good. Your stomach as fit as it looks?'

'I think so Sir.'

'Clench it then boy. I'm going to find out,' and he swung a fist lightly at me.

My body reacted of its own accord and swayed slightly as his fist just lightly grazed me but was quickly followed by his other that connected head on to knock the wind form my sails and bend me slightly over.

'I never told you to move boy. That needs punishment. Get down on the floor and clean my boots.'

I wasn't quick enough for him and the belt landed a couple of times across my shoulders before I knelt down and lowered my head to his black leather half boots.

'Get flat on the floor. Lay your slave body flat in all that mud and piss and cum so these people can see just what your body is here for.'

I lay down flat as instructed, feeling all the muck he mentioned squish under me. He raised one foot and placed it on my head, increasing the pressure until my face lay flat sidewise down and I could see his other boot just in front of my mouth.

'Start licking boy.'

I stuck my tongue out and found it would just about reach his other boot which I started to lick and clean as far as my position would allow. I half heard comments from the crowd now filling the restroom and watching my abuse.

'Gross! I wouldn't do that' 'Id fuck that ass though' 'Wonder what his mouth is like.' Wouldn't mind working that body over.'

All sorts of things like that.

'You can't do a good job like that boy. Turn over.'

He removed his foot from my head and I turned over onto my back looking straight up at a crowded ring of faces.

'Open your legs,' this was accompanied by a kick to my waist. His foot was now pressing on my balls. Squashing them against the floor. 'Is that good boy? Can you feel it?'

'Yes Sir,' I just about manage to gasp out between moans, 'Thank you.'

He lifted his foot and rested it on my stomach. 'What were we saying about your tom? Is it as strong as it looks?' applying more weight.

I was gasping, my body attempting to wriggle around and away from the pressure but to no avail. I knew my eyes were watering and could feel my face getting hot. The pressure eased.

'What will you do if I take my foot off boy?

'Anything you say Sir.'

'Anything?'

'Whatever will please you Sir. Its what I'm here for. For you.'

He'd hardly used the belt on me and not with any great force but I was already getting off on the scene. Sense and sensibility had flown out of the dirty skylight.

CHAPTER TWO

'Get up on your knees lad and open that dirty mouth of yours.'

My whole body was dripping wet and filthy from the mess on the floor but I knelt there as instructed with my head bowed down until he grabbed hold of it by the hair and wrenching it upright continued, 'Just look at these man cocks here. You will crawl up to each one and beg to suck it.'

When I didn't respond at once he slapped my head with his other hand and half dragged me forward to what looked like eight inches of fully erect manhood being rapidly given a hand job.

'Don't waste your energy man. Use this cum boys' mouth to take care of your wants. He's begging for it, aren't you boy?'

'Yes Sir. Please may I suck your cock Sir? Cum in me, or over me Sir.'

The cock I could only see out of the corner of my eyes now was placed carefully just inside my mouth and then as its owner got a little bolder slowly further and deeper until it came up against the back of my throat causing me to gag slightly. I could sense it was about to be withdrawn even though I closed my lips tightly round it but heard the man say, 'Here. Grab hold of his hair and bend his head back so you drop down easier.'

That was easy for him to say. It was my hair and my throat being attacked. The floor was hard and that cock was reacting just as it should, violating my mouth and throat, pulling in and out over my clamped lips. He was pulling my hair so hard and so far backwards I required every little brain cell still working to gasp enough oxygen through my leaking nose to remain conscious. My body felt several streams of cum and piss land on it, probably being orchestrated by the man who started to abuse me.

It was fantastic. Bang! Bang! He almost broke my nose as my hair was gripped even tighter and my face and his groin collided forcibly with each other and his cock started shooting cum; cum; cum; down my throat, filling my mouth when I was unable to swallow fast enough and leaking out from the sides to trickle down my chin. Finally his spasms finished and he pulled out, slapping his now flaccid cock back and forth across my face a few times. My original tormenters denim clad groin reappeared before me. I knew it was him because the first thing he did was backhand me across the face, left and right.

'I didn't hear you thank the nice man,' and he backhanded me again.

'Thank you for allowing me to service your cock sir.'

'That's better. Did you like it boy?'

'No Sir. This boy is here to serve, not to enjoy, he knows his place.'

That was one hell of a massive lie. I'd enjoyed every single aspect, every single second, of my abuse and degradation; all I wanted now was more of the same. It was what my body needed. What it was crying out for so deep inside where that other part of me lived, the part that could observe its hosts abuse and degradation with strangely detached enjoyment. I wanted to revel in the pain and humiliation.

'Anyone else want this lad's mouth at the moment?'

I couldn't have argued against his offer anyway as he'd grasped hold of my hair again and had one heavy boot pressing against my groin, not really hard but enough to know I'd get hurt if I tried to move. There were no immediate acceptances but someone said, 'No, but I'd sure like to piss over him while someone beats his ass. Dirty boys like him need to be punished don't they?'

'You hear that boy?' asked the man holding my hair, 'You'd better get back face down, flat on the floor so you can give the nice man what he wants.'

As usual I hesitated a moment only to receive a couple of slashes across my back with the leather belt.

'Get down there boy.'

Why is it I always hesitate? Is it because I need to be forced, or because I'm just a glutton for punishment? Bits of both I think but I'm sure to some extent it's because that part of me starting to disengage with the rest of my body takes time to transmit information back and forth. Whatever, the strokes across my back were no love taps and I cried out, even while doing as told and laying my body flat face down on the dirty wet floor. Leather booted feet appeared either side of my head.

'Head up, look forward,' and they shuffled forward, clamping my head between them with the toes pushing at my shoulders.

'Wrap your arms round my ankles boy. You better hold on tight as this is going to hurt.'

I obeyed quickly this time, pulling my body forward so my shoulders were resting on the toes of his boots, my head trapped firmly now between his ankles and wrapped my arms tightly behind his legs.

'Who wants the belt then?'

Someone must have taken it from him it as shortly I felt some love taps fall across my unprotected backside.

'Don't pussyfoot about. Whop that ass hard, that's what you want isn't it boy?'

If it pleases you sir.'

I don't know if someone else took control of the belt but the next blow landed with much more force.

Crack!

Crack!

A slight pause and I just started to breathe again when, Crack! Crack! Crack!

I yelled that time. You would have done so as well.

'Go on. Beat him again. Make him cry. Punish him. Belt him.'

All around sounded as if they were getting off and I was definitely aware of piss streams falling on my poor abused body. It seemed that as soon as one finished another took its place. Whoever had control of the belt didn't hold back any more either.

Crack! Crack! Crack! Crack! Crack!

My body was jerking and writhing around on the wet slimy floor and I held on to the legs trapping my head even tighter. My eyes were streaming, I was calling out to him, to anybody, but didn't really try to escape and only grasped his legs even tighter to my head.

'Stop, Please stop. I'll do anything you want. Don't hit me anymore. Please. Please.'

The beating finished, and I just collapsed, as far as was possible, gasping for breath with my eyes and nose streaming, I was still moaning when I had breath to spare. My front felt nearly as sore from the writhing about on the filthy floor as did my ass, but I still held tightly to the legs trapping my head.

'God that a red backside,' I heard, then felt someone's boot being placed on it and twisted across my cheeks causing me to cry out 'No', again.

'Yeah,' came from someone else, 'don't think it could take much more. Pity, it was good the way he cried and squirmed. I could use a boy like that any day.'

'There's still his back. That's still nice and white. You'd like us to whip your back boy wouldn't you?'

'Oh yes please sir. Whip boy all you want sir. Enjoy me Sir's.'

'Are you sure?' someone asked. 'Should we really be doing this to him? It must hurt.'

'I'm supposed to be hurt Sir. It's what this boy is for, what he's worth. I'll get punished later but right now he should be whipped.'

Ohoops! That was letting the cat out of the bag slightly but I don't think anyone really caught on being too busy jacking off over my dirty red assed body. It was only the feet trapping my head squeezing slightly tighter, if that was possible, that gave me any warning.

Crack! Crack! Crack! Crack!

On and on, sometimes quickly, one after the other, sometimes with a pause in between. I was yelling and throwing my body about risking damage from my contortions and contact with the floor.

'Stop! Stop! More! Flog me! Help! Don't! Go on!'

There were two quite separate persons now it seemed. One pleading for the torture to cease and the other encouraging even more and more abuse. I was yelling and crying and flying and floating. I didn't know where I was or who I was and I didn't care. I just wanted it to stop. I wanted it to continue. To go on forever, to end, never to finish.

All of a sudden the beam of a powerful torch flooded the restroom and everything stopped and all went silent.

'Well now. And just what is going on here in one of the Republics dirtiest restrooms?'

'Just a boy needing a little chastisement Sarge,' came from the man still trapping my head.

'Looks like he's been well used from here. Everyone finished with him; I'll have to take him back to the station to sort things out.'

'How long can I have Sarge?' asked the boots trapping my head.

'Fifteen long enough?' came the reply.

'Will be, I nearly shot twice already. Can I take him outside where we can see better. I want to rape his sorry red ass.'

Reaching down he grabbed the chain round my neck and jerked me upright. 'That's right ain't it boy? Your tight little ass is just begging for my hot man cock to rape it?'

I had no need to answer as he pulled my wet, dirty naked body along behind him, past the suddenly sheepish grins and downcast heads of the audience who'd only a few moments before been encouraging the abuse of my body.

'That's alright fellows,' the Sarge reassured them, 'Boys like this only fit for one thing and I can see you attended to that. I've got no problems with any of you, nothing illegal with what you been up to. Just this boy to be arrested for being naked in a public place.'

By this time I'd been led/dragged outside under the moonlight and over to a picnic table where my body was roughly flung down lengthwise.

'Grab hold the other end boy and open your legs. I'm going to stick my rod up your ass and fuck the life out of you.'

CHAPTER THREE

I was shivering slightly, it wasn't cold and I wasn't really apprehensive now. It was more a shiver of anticipation but he obviously thought otherwise, or made out he did.

'Can't have you cold boy, so let's get you warmed up then. Red ass always better anyway,' and with that he started slapping my ass with his big hand, first one cheek and then the other, slap, slap, slap, slap.

It wasn't so much the pain, I've had a belt across there often enough to know what pain is, more the surprise that had my backside moving away from his hand, 'though I still had my hands gripping the far side of the table.

'Stay still boy and he reached under me and grabbed my balls, pulling them down so any more movement became agony when he'd squeeze tighter. Finding my body now immobile he really laid into my backside this time and if I'd thought before that a hand couldn't cause pain I discovered myself to be mistaken. Very soon I could feel my cheeks burning and my body writhing on the table trapped by the grip and pull at my balls. A hand could hurt as much as a belt. My mouth was emitting groans and my eyes were streaming.

'That's better. I do like a boy in pain. Here we go then.'

His hands griped my waist, raising it slightly and in he plunged. No teasing the lips of my hole, no slow steady entrance, just Wham! Straight through my tight ass lips and on, up into my gut. My groans turned to a series of light shrieks when, having forced his entrance, he immediately turned to fucking my ass as hard as possible. His hands left my waist and made their way easily to my erect nipples as my body was arched from the table in protest at his invasion.

He pinched and twisted them, 'Hope that hurts boy. Do you like pain? I'm going to give you pain.'

His nails were digging in the tips of my nipples sending jagged streaks of agony across my pecs, I had no energy left to reply, could only twist my head back and forth, moaning and crying, gripping hard at the table edge.

'Oh I'd enjoy putting you through it boy,' he continued, 'if you think this is pain just come and visit me sometime.'

With that last comment he grabbed my body so tightly my hands lost their grasp on the table edge and we stood up momentarily, his cock firmly entrenched up my ass before being forcibly slammed back down on the table as he lost control and shot heavily, blast after blast of hot streaming cum deep inside me. It felt like a six-shooter had gone off on automatic, bang, bang, bang. For a moment he lay over me as his cock softened and slowly withdrew from my abused hole, 'I'd like you to come and visit me if you think you can take it boy.' He whispered in my ear just before he raised his weight from my back. A quick slap on my sore ass, 'Thanks anyway, take care.' And he was gone.

'You just stay there for a moment boy,' said the Sergeant as he walked back toward the restroom carrying a plastic bag. I took no real notice that my assailant accompanied him being too exhausted right then to take anything in. After a while the Sarge returned on his own showing me the bag contained my filthy soaking shorts and nipple clamps. 'Take those weights and straps off and drop them in here as well boy,' pointing at the weights still hanging from my cock. I removed that strap carefully, the wet leather had been shrinking

14

as it dried and my cock and balls had become very tender. As the circulation returned I almost wished someone would take a belt to me or something, if only to spread the pain about my body as I doubled over momentarily, clutching my balls in a vain attempt to relive them.

'You dried off yet?' he continued, 'Go get on your bike then. You can fit your boots but you won't need anything else, these shorts too wet. Can't have you catching a cold now. You know where the station is don't you. So just ride your bike in front of me and I'll follow you there, don't think of trying to escape, my bikes faster than yours.'

I had no intention of trying to escape but the thought of riding my bike through the dark night naked apart from some short boots caused a fluttering in my stomach that was nothing to do with the filth I'd swallowed earlier. On the one hand I loved my body being open to the elements and had dreamed of having a ride naked to the elements, but then it was illegal, then again I was being escorted by the local officer, and then again people might see me and they probably wouldn't be interested in the same way the fellows at the rest stop had been.

'Fire it up boy,' I had no choice.

It was the strangest feeling, riding through the early morning moonlight stark naked, my engine throbbing between my thighs, the beam of my headlamp clearing the road before me and the beam from my escort revealing every aspect of my body to any passing stranger. And there were a few of those. A couple of trucks passing the other way did a double take judging by the way their engines spluttered and one swung round and doubled back, pulling alongside the Sarge for a quick word.

Next I knew Sarge was flashing his light and in my mirror I saw him sign me to pull over. I saw a narrow turning into the woods a short way ahead and signed to turn off. The pickup followed and Sarge parked up by the roadside, which should discourage any uninvited guests. Two men got out of the pickup and I could almost see the drool running down their chins, as they looked me over. I say men but really not much more than old boys close to my own

15

age, say late teens, wearing boots, dirty torn jeans and dirty T's. The sign of light stubble on their faces and the sawdust in their cropped hair and clothes showed me they'd just finished the night shift up the wood mill.

'These two boys tell me if I'll let them have a go with you I'll find enough treated lumber in my front yard to build the deck I've been after, Seems like a good proposition to me, not really time to take you down the station now boy.'

What choice did I have? One of the lads called me to come over and I walked toward them, my balls swaying between my legs and my erect prick breaking the air before me. I've no control over that part of my anatomy, if has a mind of its own, what can I do about it?

'See you ready boy,' said number one as he pulled his T over his head, 'And you already dirty so get down there on your knees and get my cock out.'

I knelt on the muddy track and reached up to undo his belt and unzip the oil soaked cloth, which exposed a filthy smelly jock.

'Yeah! Gets a bit whiffy down there after a hard nights work, you get your mouth working there boy, suck my jock clean before I let at the real thing.'

Just in case I was having second thoughts he reached out as I knelt in the muddy track and pulled my head into his sweat and piss stinky crutch. Under the damp dirty jock I could see the outline of his thick cock laying from his balls to my right and already twitching in anticipation of my services. I gathered the saliva in my mouth and sucked and started to play that cock like a mouthorgan through his jock the vile taste of several days, if not weeks of stale sweat, piss dribbles and god knows what else swamped my mouth and my taste buds.

No way could this boy be classified as the cleanest man around. I gagged and tried unsuccessfully to pull back.

'No way boy. What you start you have to finish. That's what my old man always tells me so don't make him out to be a liar.'

With that his changed his grip from holding the back of my head to gripping my hair so any movement in retreat now tore at my roots, 'Go on now, you suck away and save me having to wash them and maybe, just maybe, I'll let you pull them down and get your sweet lips round my snake.'

His jock was rank and all I could do was work on his cock in the hope he'd soon want something a little more direct. Meanwhile, his companion had been getting himself in the mood and somewhat to my relief I heard, 'Come on Joe, I've not got all morning to muck about and this here is wanting to blow soon. Anyway, you know how Mother gets riled if we don't get home before she leaves. Let me fuck that mouth for a bit if you don't want to.'

My hair was released and the body standing before me replaced by number two. This was a different kettle of fish. Already jeans and jock dropped to boots and shirt removed with a good six or seven inch uncut member standing proud and ready with a pair of nicely rounded balls puckering up underneath. I rather enjoyed the view for a moment but returning to my situation slid forward and engulfed him straight down, twisting my head at just the right moment allowed him full access without causing me to gag.

I knew that it was the earlier workout my mouth had suffered that eased his entrance and his remark earlier about his father's homily brought one of my mothers to mind, every cloud has a silver lining. Thinking that almost caused me to choke after all, this time though from laughter. He really was getting ready to blow soon I could tell from the throbbing and swelling from his cock inside my mouth, but that wasn't really a surprise as he appeared to be only a couple of years older than myself and I seemed ready and willing at the drop of a hat, several times a day.

'God, he's good,' came a breathless voice, better than that slut in the wages office, or that fellow we met at the truck stop. This one really knows how to service a cock, almost convince enough to turn me gay if I'd get service like this every time.'

He was thrusting away by now, in and out of my clenched lips and slightly upturned face, with just a light hand resting on my head. We were both dancing to the same tune. I kept getting flashes of his washboard stomach with just a light sprinkling of almost downy hair round he cute little belly button each time he pulled back and from the corner of my eye saw his brother had now also striped down and beating his meat furiously. I will admit to an enjoyment of my position, also of the cock I was servicing and brought my hands up to fondle and pull lightly on his matched set of balls causing an outbreak of swearing, especially when I slowed my head and allowed my teeth to lightly nibble toward the end of his cock.

His reactions to my services were too much for his brother who calling out, 'Yes, Yes, Yes,' and other things I didn't catch, was suddenly shooting streams of cum over my face and his brothers stomach.

'Hell Jo!' he said, you've cum everywhere, I'm soaked with it.

'Well, wouldn't be the first time bro, just get your boy there to lick it off when you've done.'

That was enough for my other young assailant as placing both hands on my head to hold it steady three rapid face fucks had him repeating his brother and shooting his load, in this case, straight down my throat at first and then as he slowed, filling my mouth. I'm not ageist, couldn't afford to be the way I like cock, but, there is something about a young cock and it contents, both in texture and in taste that just hits the right spot. In other circumstances I'd happily serviced that stud for the rest of the day but duty called. When I'd fully finished milking him and he pulled out saying with a laugh, 'you can't take it home,' I raised my head and started licking his brothers cum from his stomach.

'Just look at that,' the brother said, 'I bet he'd take our piss as well if Sarge told him to.'

'You haven't got time,' Sarge came back with, 'get him up and face down over your pickup hood, I'm going to have the boys ass.'

'Hell Sarge' said number 2, 'You'll never get that up without killing him. I never knew you were that huge.'

'That's why you two will have to hold his arms either side so he can't get away. Then you can piss over him after.'

That last convinced them, they wanted to piss over me I suppose, anyway, my arms were quickly grabbed and my body flung over the still warm hood of their pickup and one brother stood either side holding my outstretched arm. I heard Sarge spit and spit again to lube his cock and felt him stick a finger up my ass to see if any natural lubrication remained from my recent fucking. Even though it had been a while I could feel a small residue of ass slime and cum leak out as his fingers checked and removing them to wipe over my back he said, 'That will have to do,' and rapidly forced an entry.

My body took off and would have gone into orbit if not for being restrained by the brothers. It didn't take off for joy but in shock and an attempt to escape the abuse. He was huge. I was too shocked to scream, my feet actually left the ground which in retrospect made things worse, being unable to actual levitate, my body had to return and in so doing became more firmly impaled on his monster. Sarge was long enough to be fun but it was his width that caused me such anguish. Even though I'd been so thoroughly fucked earlier this was splitting me apart.

'Get it out! Get it out!' I was yelling.

The boys keeping tight hold of my outstretched wrists were grinning and laughing to Sarge to 'Rape him! Fuck him!' and the Sarge just told me to 'Hold on boy. Here we go.'

Fuck! Here we did go, well he did anyway. I was unlikely to be going anywhere for a bit, spread-eagled over the pickups hood under the early morning sun starting to percolate through the branches. Sarge got going though, in my ass. Humping and fucking, stretching my hole. There being solid metal under my stomach forcing the air from my lungs with every painful thrust. I would never have thought I'd get to enjoy being fucked by a cock as broad as his but actually my body was responding as usual because I felt my cock attempt to stand proud under me, which actually made matters worse seeing as how it was trapped under my stomach and was also being squeezed painfully at each plunge. His hands reached up to grab my head and was lightly slamming it up and down on the hard metal as he unloaded in my ass, thoroughly re-filling the abused area to the brim and then, being still plugged by his half-hard member, leaking and running down my legs.

'That's how to make use of a boy like this,' the Sarge remarked, 'But, if I ever hear of you two using any other girl, or boy, like it I'll be down on you like a ton of bricks. I just knew this one was ready for it. Weren't you boy?'

Pulling out he reached down and catching a handful of the mess escaping from my wide-open hole reached up and wiped it over my face and mouth. 'Oh yes! You were ready,' slathering another handful over my erect cock and bruised balls on display as he pulled me upright. 'Oh well. You better get down on your back so these boys can have a piss before they get of home hadn't you?'

Pushing me reasonably gently till I ended laying on the muddy track, face up, legs bent and wide apart, my aching cock waving in the breeze. Sarge stood between my legs and after a moment his massively thick member unloaded a hosepipe of piss over my raised legs, cock, balls and stomach.

'Go on boys, you can use the other end. Make him open his mouth and swallow.'

As first one, and then two thin streams of piss started to play over my closed eyes and chest one asked, 'How do we do that Sarge?'

'Like this,' and I felt a heavy thick boot placed over my privates and start slowly to press and grind.

Of course I opened my mouth, there were now threes streams of piss playing over me and even as my mouth filled the boot increased pressure, squeezing my frustrated bits and pieces and I came. Oh yes! I shot, and shot, and shot. Everywhere. Even through the dying piss streams I could feel it land over my face and chest and still the boot continued to twist and still I continued to shoot.

Finally, thank God, everything came to an end. My filthy soaking body was too exhausted to move and just lay on the muddy track as I heard Sarge tell the lads to get off home, and then, with a grin as he dropped my still wet shorts across my crotch. 'Get yourself dressed boy and off home before someone finds you here and arrests you for indecency,' That was one of the best yet. You know what to do next time you decide you have to visit a rest stop to play?'

'I'll text you time and place of course Sarge. Don't I always.'

'You do boy. By the way, I've stuck a card on your handlebars from that colored gent who had your ass earlier. He says to text your mobile number if you want. I know him slightly and think he's safe, though bit more advanced than you. Has to be your decision. Got to go. You OK?'

I nodded. Quite frankly I was so psyched I'd almost be ready for another session but still had a sixty mile ride home in my filthy state and had to get going. I found the card Sarge mentioned when putting my T and jacket on. On one side a mobile number, on the other four words in a rough print.

I'LL HURT YOU BOY

CHAPTER FOUR

There was something about that card and its terse message that hit a cord somewhere but I knew and trusted the Sarge, I didn't know this man apart from that one session in a dirty restroom with others to intervene if necessary. I almost threw it away and then when I finally got home, washed up and recovered, found myself searching frantically for it, finally texting my mobile number before falling into a deep sleep where I dreamed of Darth Vader calling out, 'Come here boy and sit on this.' My problem was that with the lousy lighting and his black costume I just couldn't make out what I had to sit on and woke with my body laying in a wet messy patch. What a waste, I'd just had a wet dream.

Nothing happened for the rest of that week and I'd decided it had to be a wind up when I got a text message, 'when are you free for two nights boy?'

I replied, 'not for two weeks. Friday pm to Sunday pm.' Before I gave myself time to think.

Did I really want to follow this up, I almost sent a follow up to cancel the last when I received, 'You will call me Sir boy. It's the least of what you'll be calling me in two weeks.'

Well. I could always back out later, say I was ill or something and this texting might be fun. There continued over the next week a series of texts during which he uncovered my place and hours of work, that I lived alone, that I was not really that experienced just always randy and a whole load of other stuff I never realized I let out. When the second week started his texts changed. Now he was telling me what to do, just little things like stick a plug up my ass and a strap round my cock, and then take the rubbish out in a pair of skimpy running shorts.

I obeyed the first but wore my usual shorts to discover a text waiting the moment I walked back through my door, 'I said running shorts boy.' Followed by, 'If you can't do a simple thing like that I'll find someone else.'

Suddenly I didn't want him to find someone else; I was getting involved in this strange relationship almost against my will. Tearing into the bedroom I tore my shorts and T off replacing them with just the skimpy runners and rushed back outside, bending over facing the house as if to pick up some rubbish, with my ass in the air and showing the bulge from the plug if anyone had wanted to look. I waited as long as possible, even chatting to a neighbor for a moment who must have wondered at my mode of dress then returned inside, hardly daring to check my phones display.

'OK boy, this time. You won't get another second chance. Same again tomorrow but with full bladder around eight, I'll text.'

Eight? It would only just be dusk; anyone going by would see everything. Why was I hard as hell, I grasped my cock and a couple of squeezes had me shooting inside my shorts. He was keeping me aroused every waking moment. I'd just cum and wanted to start again. The next evening, the last before I was supposed to visit him, by eight I was clothed as he'd instructed, same as previous night but this with a uncomfortable bladder. I wasn't even sure I wanted to go through tonight's little charade, let alone visit for a weekend. Ten past eight I was starting to squeeze my cock in a vain attempt to ease the pressure. That's it, I told myself. I'm being messed around. He won't come. Just go and piss in the bathroom. Forget him. My legs were almost crossed, the phone buzzed.

'Now,' it said, 'bring the phone with you.'

I hobbled rather than ran to the front yard, then toward the bins. For the first time I noticed a dark colored small truck parked over the street with darkened windows in the rear section. Was he there? I played toward the truck anyway and then stood beside my gatepost as if looking down the street. Ding. A text.

'Let it go boy.'

Have you ever tried to piss standing in a public street in the twilight, your cock and balls strapped up, a plug up your ass and just wearing a pair of running shorts. Even though my bladder was bursting I just couldn't make it start. Ding.

'Crouch down and pull the plug from your ass boy.'

This was mad. Even so I obeyed. It was admittedly a small plug and popped out readily when I managed to get my hand inside the waistband and returning to an upright position I discovered the flow had already started. Flow? More like a gushing torrent soaking my thin shorts and flooding down my legs and trainers to pool under my feet. After a while the truck moved off, I never saw anyone move into the drives seat, and I waited a moment longer before making a very careful journey back indoors glad I'd thought to leave an old towel just inside the door. I only had time to strip what little I wore when Ding.

'You may just do boy. Have to see. Don't wash shorts or trainers, bring with you tomorrow. Expect call when you finish work. That will be your last chance to back out. I WILL HURT YOU.'

That night Darth Vader was joined by crowds of storm troopers in leather straps pissing over me and telling me to let it go. This time I woke to discover I'd soaked the whole bed with piss, luckily always made up with a rubber under sheet for solo play and only had time to strip the sheets, start the wash cycle and have a quick shower before off to work. No time for a wank, quick or slow and that I really did needed. I never got my erection to go down all day and by the time four came round was fed up with comments from the other staff not to mention being in receipt of a slightly sore tip from all the rubbing it had received in my jock.

Five minutes past, I'd only just got to the changing room and picked up my phone to check when Ding. 'Change. You don't need jock or T. Ride to... and I'll call'.

It was difficult to hide from my fellow workers that I'd removed my jock but somehow I managed to get my denim cut-offs over my package, then socks and boots followed by just my leather jacket. 'No T?' someone asked. 'Too hot,' I replied.

They were used to me dressing a bit odd as they called it and I got away with that. Purring down the main roads, then off on a couple of side ones warm wind caressing my chest and up the legs of my shorts did nothing to ease the excitement rumbling bin my groin. When I got to... all I wanted to do was rip my fly open and jerk off violently. I think I would have done but that bloody phone went again.

Ding. 'Quarter mile down road wood frame house well set back on left. Drive into open garage. Strip. Leave clothes on bike. Wear trainers and carry run shorts. Come and knock on door. This is your last chance boy. Once in you stay until Sunday afternoon.'

Why didn't I reconsider? My cock led me; I had no control over that. Also, in retrospect, he'd played me like a master should. Well, I suppose he was one of sorts, just not my type but I had still to discover that. He'd become mine for that weekend and I followed his instructions exactly. I found the house without much problem and rode in to the double garage containing another bike and the black van I'd half expected. As I walked back out, quite naked apart from the dirty trainers and carrying the shorts I heard the door slide down behind me. The house was set back from a side road with several trees to shield me, even so I felt quite exposed as I rang the doorbell. I had to wait several minutes the door opened, he stood before me and I got my first real look at the man who might be changing my life.

Very dark as I'd seen before, around six foot so slightly taller than me, close cropped crinkly hair, both eyes and glistening teeth standing out in a frowning face, followed down by a body at least twice a broad as my own, everywhere, but without an ounce of fat to be seen. Washboard stomach, biceps, thighs, bulge in tight

25

cotton shorts, all huge, but somehow not extreme, his body was all beautifully in proportion. He looked down at me from the doorstep and without warning lashed out with one open hand sending me sprawling to the ground.

'Boys like you don't call at front doors. Go round the back and sit on the ground where you belong, also drink the two bottles of water you find there while you wait for me. I'll be out when ready.'

He closed the door with a slam, not waiting to see if I obeyed. What else could I do, my bike and clothes were locked in his garage, all I had were the dirty little shorts I carried so I rose to me feet and trudged carefully round to the back, tears running down my face. But how much they were tears of pain, how much expectation and how much of despondency I couldn't say. My prick was still hard.

CHAPTER FIVE

I discovered two bottles of cold water standing under what looked at first appearance to be a frame for climbing plants but as I sat down cross legged and looked closer it was obviously far too strong being made of six by six, not to mention the rings bolted through at different places and the fact I was sitting on a solid concrete concave slab with a drain hole in the centre. Were it not for the small section of carpet tile I sat on my backside would have been burning from the reflected heat.

He'd not told me I couldn't look around so I observed this was situated a large, obviously secluded, tree and grass-dominated garden leading from the fair sized half roofed patio. I could only hazard a guess as to the house but estimated it as probably three bedroom and all that went with that, after all he had a large double garage I'd been in and what looked like another single garage that built on the other side that for some reason had its door facing the garden.

It surprised me to discover I'd drunk both large bottles of water and my tears had quite finished falling when I became aware of a pair of lightly haired very dark legs clad just in flip flops appear before me. I went to look up and had just caught sight of those cotton shorts with their massive bulge when another almighty slap to my head knocked me to the ground.

'Never raise your head to me unless I tell you to,' he said, 'when I do you may wish I hadn't'

Then his massive hand reached down under my chin to turn my face upwards, 'No tears this time I see!'

Did he see everything?

'Stand up and keep your head down.' I stood. 'Bladder filling boy?'

'Yes Sir.' It wasn't that uncomfortable but there was a pressure there.

'Close your eyes boy,' he put a blindfold over them anyway and then was fastening what I recognized as padded straps round my wrists and ankles, also a solid metal ring round my balls to which he attached a light weight.

'That weight stays on all weekend boy. I'll add or remove others as I see fit.'

My body was trembling when he held my now almost flaccid cock and tried to do something with the piss slip. When had my cock gone down? When he blindfolded me so I was unable to see what he would do?

'This won't do. Get down flat on your back and stop shaking; I'm not going to cut it off or anything.'

I managed to lay down with his assistance and for the first time in my life had someone slide a small plastic tube up my piss slit and then strap both my cock and the tube to my stomach so they wouldn't come apart.

'Now get up and come over here.'

It wasn't easy but with his arms to guide me I sort of shuffled in the direction he wanted and found my body being bent face down at the waist over some apparatus that allowed him to fasten off my wrist and ankles and left my ass, so I thought, stuck in the air at just the right angle for fucking or worse. Those parts of my body not restricted by the straps he was now fastening round me were trembling, part in anticipation but also in some trepidation. What had I got myself into?

'I just get off on hurting boys like you and letting others do the same and that's what will happen this weekend. I'm not into twenty-four seven relationships or anything and whether you come back or not is quite up to you. However, this weekend you will get hurt and probably auctioned off and I will enjoy every moment. Your enjoyment is of no concern to me.'

Just as I was about to raise some objections he forced a rubber ball gag in my mouth and fastened it off behind my head, which by now was about the only part of my body I could move.

'Breathe through your nose,'

I'd not even realized there was an air hole through the gag till he plugged it, I discovered soon, with the tube stuck up my prick.

'Hope you ready boy,' as a belt landed across my backside. 'Cant damage that too much, may want to sell it off later,' and the belt was landing across my back instead.

Not regularly or always with the same force, but it just kept on coming. I'd had my backside belted before but never really my back and certainly never like this and with the ball gag I was also unable to yell or scream. Have you ever been flogged when quite unable to move, not from fear but restricted so tightly you couldn't move any part of your body apart from your head, and also unable to squeeze more than a whimper past your gags when all you wanted to do was scream and swear and jerk about and escape.

I would have done anything just then to make him stop, not almost anything, but absolutely anything. My eyes weren't just crying, they were the Niagara Falls, I was in agony. Worse was to come. Through the gag came a liquid I recognized with some horror as piss. I knew. I was pissing in my own mouth. No problem, I'd done it before. The problem this time was that I had no awareness of releasing my bladder. That tube he'd stuck up my piss slit had taken away all feeling apart from some bloating and I had no control over what my bladder would do.

Strangely enough the first feeling when he stopped beating me was more one of loss rather than relief, but was only until the pain really set in. I never struggled at all when he untied me, removed the blindfold and stood me under the wood frame, raising my arms above my head and attaching them to a couple of chains, then knocking my legs apart doing much the same to them.

His face only a foot or so from mine his fingers found my nipples. 'Have you been drinking boy?' I nodded. 'Seem to have run out,' he continued and fumbled about down below, 'Be some more soon.' Did I hurt you?' I nodded again. 'Did you enjoy it?' as he pinched and twisted my nipples?' I shook my head.

'Too bad. Do you want some more?' I nodded.

I nodded!!! Tears were still streaming down my cheeks and when he left of torturing my nipples and slid his hands over my back my body almost passed out with shock. Yet I agreed to more.

'Just have this little drink first then boy.' His face screwed up slightly as if he were concentrating hard and after a moment a fresh stream of fresh piss swamped my mouth. Somehow he'd connected his own cock to the tube and had enough pressure on board to force a stream up the tube to my mouth. His fingers returned to my nipples,

'Drink deep boy.' What choice did I have? I heard a phone ringing in the distance and with,' Hang around will you,' and a light slap he moved back to the house.

Again a remark I had little choice but to obey strung up as I was. He returned carrying a spray can to tell me, 'You can have a five minute rest. Couple of boys I know on their way who will enjoy hurting you on my behalf. Just as much fun to watch as to indulge. They'll want sex as well, more than once if I remember correctly, but you won't mind that will you?'

He shook the can and sprayed the freezing contents my burning back. For a moment it felt even worse, if that was possible, but then did seem to ease the pain to a dull throb. Then he was back to look into my glaring eyes, 'Well you've not said no so obviously you agree to the lads joining in.'

He grinned while slapping my dick back and forth a few times. 'I think I'll let them unplug your cock, that will give them another part of your body to play with. Pity if we leave any area out don't you think?'

He roughly squeezed some cool cream or grease round the lips and slightly inside my hole and then with a comment of, 'Push out,' thumped my stomach with one hand causing my body to try and double over, while with the other rammed a butt plug straight in and up inside me. If I'd not been strung up I know I would have tried to hit him. That wasn't pain. It was agony. I'd been split apart.

He attached some sort of belt that fitted tightly round my waist, then a strap down my crack and up either side of my balls, finally being clipped on the waist strap. That held the plug firmly in position not to mention was squeezing the side of my balls. 'Just one more thing,' and he pulled painfully on my balls, attaching a strap round them and leaving them stretched out. Standing up he looked back in my face, 'Now that wasn't so bad was it?'

Actually, now the initial stretching had eased the plug felt quite at home, it was the straps keeping everything tight that were more uncomfortable but even those I could bear for a while. His fingers returned to my nipples and he grinned as I flinched, 'I asked you if it was too much to put up with? I take it the answer is no sir. That's good.'

Reaching behind me he took a couple of slaps at my backside, 'God I'd love to have a go at that but I can get more for it if reasonably undamaged. Don't worry, I'll have my go when I get you back.'

CHAPTER SIX

I heard a vehicle pull up out front, followed shortly by doors slamming, laughing voices coming round the other garage and then, almost as shocked as I was, the two young men Big Sarge had allowed to use me briefly a couple of weeks back.

'Now that's a nice surprise, been looking all over for you,' one of them said, 'Told you we'd enjoy a longer session and it looks like we going to get one now, and then some.'

The other asked. 'What can we do with him?' when turning to my host.

'Whatever you like,' he replied. 'Just leave his backside alone for now. I'm going to take him to the truck park later and auction it off. You can fuck it though, just plug him after, you know how they like a dirty ass down there.'

'Can we take his gag out? We like to hear and anyway will need his mouth anyway.'

'OK. Better use the den, sound travels too far this time of day. Take his piss tube out as well. He can drink from the tap in future.'

How long had I been here? It was already turning dusk, and what did he mean about auctioning my backside? They unclipped my restraints and led me into the other garage. Once inside and the door closed I discovered it to be laid out for torture, not storing motor vehicles. The whole place was painted black apart from red tile paint covering the floor. The two lads must have been here before as they rushed round quickly flicking switches and lighting candles bathing the whole room in soft red flickering light apart from some mini white spots over the equipment in the centre. When that got lit up I almost turned to go, even dressed as I was, or wasn't.

Too late. My host was standing right behind holding a camcorder in one hand and easily catching and holding me with the other.

'I told you once in, no change of mind. What about my friends here anyway, they've come all this way for a bit of fun and now they've found you here to play with they can really go to town. Not to mention I should get a film out of this I can sell for more than all of their other ones put together.

'I don't know what would have happened if I'd made a real effort to get away then. I will admit to being scared as to what might or would happen but there was also this other side that wanted to endure, to take anything he could throw at me, the same side of me that would visit dirty rest stops in the middle of the night dressed in little more than the straps I wore now. Also in the back of my mind was the fact Big Sarge had some idea of where I'd gone and would go looking if I didn't call him from time to time.

Even so, I was shaking when they came for me. The lads had striped right off and now wore little more than studded leather jocks, some odd bits of chain and harness, their original boots, and a couple of small eye masks. I recognized the dress and bodies now from a couple of very vanilla S&M films I'd seen, very vanilla but nice as background for the bodies of the two lads who jerked off for the camera. I'd liked the look of them when Sarge gave them a quick go at me; I'd thought then a longer session might be fun. I'd just not been thinking of the type of session it seemed was about to occur.

My host pushed me toward them and I just made out the whir of his camcorder starting, then forgot all about him as they lit into me with hardly a word. One grabbed my shoulders from behind and spun me round to face the cam while the other punched me in the stomach, not quite as hard as it could have been but sufficient to knock the wind out of me and with the other pushing my shoulders I realized I should fold down to the floor. Once down there they wasted little time and fewer words strapping my wrists together, pulling a chain down from the roof to attach them to, then two further chains they attached to each ankle.

Bending to my head the ball gag was removed from my mouth and while I was licking and swallowing to clear my mouth, the tube stuck up my prick was jerked out without warning. I yelled, for a split second it was an indescribable pain, gone almost at once, just leaving a memory of hell as I heard a clanking and found my legs were being raised from the floor by a hoist that just kept on turning, my legs stretched apart, till my whole body was hanging upside down, my head lying at right angles on the smooth painted floor.

'If we can't warm his ass outside, how about inside?' one of the lads asked my host.

'Don't see why not.'

It wasn't the expected cock that followed a shot of cold grease up my hole however but several fingers, forcing their way straight through my ass lips and turning to twist and pull inside my hole. My body was twisting and scraping against the floor in protest at the invasion and abuse and my mouth was keeping them good company.

'Let's shut him up for a while,' followed by that clanking again and discovering my arms were being pulled up by the chain attached to my bound wrists very shortly followed by my body as the clanking continued.

Soon I discovered myself hanging from outstretched legs and combined arms a few feet from the floor. It was difficult to hold my head up but I did see a thinner choke chain fitted behind my balls and attached overhead where, when it was released, some weight was applied to assist the stretching my balls. My head fell back as it was too much effort to hold it up and I couldn't see what else they were doing to me. Next were fingers prizing my mouth open to fit a solid rubber covered ring just behind my teeth with straps fastened off behind my head.

I knew what its use was but had only seen one before; never had one fitted or thought it would be needed. I was wrong. Only a moment later a cock was fed through the ring and part way down my throat accompanied by fingers twisting and pinching my nipples.

'This is one face fuck you won't forget in a hurry.'

Apart from my body being hung up and my head falling toward the floor it didn't seem that different so far. The fingers invading my ass were removed and wiped over my chest, shortly to be replaced by the warm solid rod of an aroused cock forcing a violent entrance and not stopping until fully home. This of course swung my body to make my mouth engulf the cock there down to its bush the gag reflex passing quickly due to the angle of my neck. Breathing was difficult, the cocks filling my mouth and ass were not moving as normal which would have eased the situation, the fingers attacking my nipples were removed and a voice

'Now.'

My body went into spasms, upward, sideways, crashing back down against the chains and back up again as what felt like a pair of prongs were stuck against my body, again and again. My thighs, my sides, my stomach, just once on my groin, that was the worse. Pure unadulterated agony. All the time those cocks spit roasting me from either end remained static, it was the gyrations of my body working on them that caused the increase of blood, that caused them to swell even larger, to throb to heat up. They were however pushing harder and deeper inside me,

'More. Do him again. Increase the dose. Go on, hurt him.'

They were the sort of comments I could hear above an almost continuous moaning that were coming from my own mouth, escaping round that plug of a cock. I sounded almost inhuman; the state my body was being subjected to right then was inhuman. Shock; after shock; after shock.

'Enough,' came a shout and the attack ceased as the cock filling my mouth was withdrawn and rapidly wanked off over my face. 'Don't waste it,' and a hand scraped the resulting mess into my mouth while holding my head upright by its hair.

Shortly after the cock in my ass did the same, shooting over my stomach and feeding me the consequence after finally removing the mouth ring. They let my body down to lie limply on the cold floor. I couldn't have moved to save my life. When someone said they wanted a piss and I had to return outside I didn't even respond when being kicked in the side and finally was picked up by my arms and legs, carried out to a muddy area when they just dropped me and pissed all over my body. I didn't, just couldn't, care. The pain had ceased but my body was still in denial and withdrawal. It was only when I saw raw footage a few weeks later I became aware the boys had only maintained contact with my body with their cocks, their hands holding the chains above my body, while the camera man, my original abuser, kept on poking my body with a battery powered cattle rod.

No wonder I made no response when first released, still made little reaction when moved, hosed down, carried to and laid face down in the back of that dark windowed truck I'd seen before, my face toward the rear door. Even when they all climbed in the cab and the vehicle started to move I was only just starting to recover. I'd forgotten. He'd said he was going to sell my ass!

CHAPTER SEVEN

I must have actually dozed off or possibly passed out and only came to when I felt the vehicle pull quickly to a stop and the cab doors open and slam close. I was still lying on my stomach facing the rear doors when they were flung open and a subdued light flooded in.

'Hell, he ain't joking. He had got a lad with a tight pert ass laying out here. How much to fuck it did you say?'

There was a fair amount of whispering and grumbling then my original abuser climbed in and after raising my groin to shove what felt, and smelt, like an old dirty tarp underneath pointing my backside up in the air, clipped the wrist and ankle straps still attached to rings conveniently placed in each corner of the van.

'Right. He's ready now, which ones first?'

'What if he yell's? Don't want too much attention.'

'He won't,' bending down to look in my face, 'you know better than to make too much noise don't you?' accompanied by a couple of slaps. 'Just to be safe though,' he reached into the corner and pulling my head up let it fall back down on a rank piss soaked rag.

'That's my old piss and cum filled jock. If he gets too loud just shove that in his mouth. We're off to get a takeaway, don't take too long.'

Fuck him! He'd left me at the mercy of a bunch of strangers who could do almost anything they wanted and any objections on my part would only result on being gagged by the rank rag lying under my face. This wasn't going to be like my own trips out to be fucked where I did at least have some control over what abuse would happen to my body. One of the groins standing round in front of the open door stepped forward, for that was all my view allowed, a series of dirty overalls, jeans and a few shorts from thigh to stomach against the shadowed light. He pulled a thick flaccid uncut cock through the gap of his overalls.

'Suck on this lad. You better get it nice and wet before I use it to plug your sweet tight ass hole.'

Well, I may not be quite as sweet or tight as he thought but could see what was hanging there would not find an easy entrance however much I licked and lubed. Even hanging down in its semi limp state what I saw was not a normal prick by any description. It had to be at least eight inches long and I'd never close my fingers round it now, let alone when it woke up. Even Big Sarge would have looked small beside it. He stuck a small brown bottle under my nose.

'Take a big long sniff lad, it should help.'

Poppers, thank god! I'd soon need all the help I could get. While he held my head loosely and started to wipe his rapidly hardening cock along my lips as if I was playing a mouth organ I felt the van bounce as a couple of people clambered in alongside me.

'Are you sure this is OK pop? We can just fuck this ass and no comebacks?'

'You saw me pay the man didn't you? That ass belongs to us for the next thirty minutes and I need you two getting it ready for me. Strip off and fuck boys, I know you love an audience.'

I didn't get to see what his sons looked like right then but judging him as under forty would put them as no more than twenty and it was obvious they did like an audience and the van jiggled around some more as I guessed they were striping off and then, with no warning, several fingers were brutally shoved straight in my hole. I yelped and tried to pull my body away from the invasion.

'He's wet but still tight pop. Shouldn't need any more lube.'

'You warn me before doing that again boys; I was just about to find out how welcoming his mouth was. You oil him up good anyway; He'll need all the help he can get when I take your place.'

It felt as if a whole tube of some thick cold grease or cream was injected in my ass then, 'here I go,' was followed by a stiff cock wasting no time in plunging straight down and up to the hilt. The feeling of that thick grease being pushed deep inside my gut was like shitting in reverse, most peculiar. I must have made some sound as the massive cock asked, 'you like that then lad?'

Actually I did. The cock was a nice warm rod that fitted perfectly and was now sliding slowly in and out with a natural rhythm I tried to meet. Also, the feeling when the grease started warming up and coating all my whole gut rather than just the usual ass lips was somehow rather soothing.

'Yes, thought you'd like my boys. They do a good ass fuck, can keep it up all night between them but we've not got the time. Pity, you've a much better body than most of the boy's I buy them.'

He used his fingers to pry my mouth open and stuck the tip of his cock between me teeth, 'It's all right. I'm not going to fuck your pretty little face lad; I'd have to knock all your teeth out for that. No reason you shouldn't suck on me for a bit though.'

Actually, once my mouth managed to accommodate his girth and the knowledge, hopefully truth, that he wouldn't be trying to get that weapon down my throat, did leave no reason why I shouldn't be sucking away. I was in fact quite enjoying myself. The cock up my ass had increased its speed and could be felt almost sloshing around now that whatever grease had been used was warmed up. He was actually a good fucker, big enough to feel without massive pain, good steady and increasing stroke, and his hands gripping my upper thighs to obtain better grip and angle. He was fucking my ass and intent on his own pleasure, in the process pleasuring me as well.

I sucked happily on the fathers weapon, almost forgetting where it would be later as my body surrendered to the attack on my rear. It was, of course, too good to last. The cock up my ass speeded up and unloaded almost without my notice as his thrusts forced more of the father's weapon in my mouth and hitting the back of my throat. Both cocks were withdrawn at almost the same time and my ass was penetrated again, but this time by a considerably larger object and one quite prepared to ram my body through the floor of the van. It was a good thing my mouthful had been removed as I had some trouble not to allow more than the odd whimper or groans escape through my lips. This boy knew he was hurting me and obtaining enjoyment from the fact.

'Take it lad,' came from the body before my face, 'He's just opening you up for me. Do you want gagging?'

I shook my head. I had no wish for the soaking and stinking filthy jock at present under my chin to be jammed in my mouth. Apart from anything else I'd have to swallow some of the contents and even just smelling it made me retch. So I took it. Actually, once my body got over the initial forced entry it wasn't too bad. His problem was that he thought the only way to hurt me lay in a forced fuck and I'd been forced, fucked and hurt by experts. He needed training in how to sexually abuse a body and I felt disinclined to assist. At least he was opening my hole somewhat in preparation for the assault to come. He wasted so much energy and concentration in showing the audience how good he was that he started shooting before he wanted. I heard him.

'Shit! Fuck! Too soon!' And he didn't leave much of a deposit either.

'How was he?' the father asked me, causing the truck to tip to one side as he clambered aboard.

'Waste of time,' I replied. Probably a stupid remark in my present circumstances but he was. His brother earlier had actually done a better job of preparing my hole for the violation about to occur. My smart remark resulted in a fist alongside my head from one of the boys exiting the truck and a follow-up comment from the father.

'You leave him alone now, you've had your turn and he only said what I've told you before when I share a boy with you.' Then, with a change of tone, 'You just try and relax lad, one of you boys popper him up, he's about to get royally fucked.'

The welcome bottle appeared under my nose to be gratefully inhaled. I'd seen what was already probing at the rosebud of my hole, I'd even felt part of it in my mouth, and still couldn't believe it was about to force its way inside and up my gut. There was no way my hole could stretch for that. It tried though; I'll give it that. He pushed hard at my hole and as I held my breath I actually thought for a moment he'd break through, but no. Even so it hurt.

'Feed him more poppers, he's got to relax more.' The bottle reappeared, this time accompanied by a young face surrounded by damp wiry hair and the most kissable lips.

'You have to let him in. He get there one way or another, what can I do to help?'

'Poppers, and kiss me when he tries again please.'

Where did I get the cheek to ask that? This family, and the audience I'd almost forgotten about, had to be as hetro and butch as possible. I'd get my head kicked in for that. Now that I considered it there were voices all around, jostling for space and a view into the truck of my spread-eagled body and the monster cock about to split me.

'Go on. Fuck the cunt. Rape that boy ass. Make him yell,' and other like comments surrounded us.

The bottle, the feelings of a baseball bat at my rear, and, two hands holding my head and from nowhere it seemed a set of lips clamped tightly against mine. What actually caused my body to allow an entrance I have no idea but I couldn't ignore the fact that something had invaded my ass, something broader than it had ever experienced before. Something that still intended to reach depths never violated before.

CHAPTER EIGHT

Thank god for that little bottle. I'd inhaled deeply the moment my hole flinched away from its massive attacker but that alone didn't account for the fact I'd not screamed the place down when the initial violation occurred, let alone as my body was slowly but surely invaded by that monster weapon. I was split in half and then quarters by the slow but steady invasion, I wanted to scream but my lips were sealed and my breath taken by the lips so impossibly clamped to mine, the tongue boldly playing touch and go with my own

Even when I felt his ball sac and hairy groin slam against my poor ass cheeks he hadn't finished. Reaching down to pry my cheeks further apart he rammed that extra half-inch of his weapon in, nailing my lower body to the floor. As his hands moved again, this time to grip my shoulders the upper section of my body was flexing and writhing in a vain effort to escape his attack, but of course just allowing his cock easier access and movement.

As he started slowly, very slowly thank God, to slide in and out, back and forth, he had the accompaniment of voices from outside that I'd almost forgotten about under the assault to encourage him.

'Yeah. Go for it. Fuck the little bastard. Rape his ass. Split him,' and such, plus other suggestions for future use I tried to filter out. As he started, the mouth that had kissed me so deeply changed to a pair of hands holding my head firmly, and a soft warm voice.

'Try to go with it, relax and enjoy.'

How the hell could I enjoy being fucked, no raped, by that monster of a cock?

'Go on,' the voice continued, take it and feed on the pain. You know you want to really.'

As the speed of my assault increased slightly I realized the voice was right, how could he know me better that I did myself? Finally I managed to open my eyes. It was difficult to see much against the lights from outside, untidy shoulder length hair, a smiling young face about my own age and a pair of deep dark eyes looking straight into mine.

'It's getting to you now, I just knew he would but I fucked you first. How was I?'

'Lovely,' I managed to gasp as my attacker speeded up again.

'Did I hurt you?' I nodded.

'You enjoyed it?' I nodded again.

'And now?'

'Different? I'd rather it be you any time.'

'What about every night?' he asked.

'Would you punish me?' I asked.

Where was this conversation coming from, more to the point, where was it going?

'Every time I feel like it,' he answered. 'You'll move in with me and work in our garage. Ma won't mind, she knows how I am and there won't be any little bastard's turning up in your case! Apart from me that is! He grinned. 'Anytime I want your ass I'll take it, it will be all mine. I'll may farm your mouth out though.'

The cock up my ass was really pounding now, my front was going to be black and blue from the punishment it was getting from the van floor. I couldn't concentrate on what he was saying anymore, all I could feel, all I knew, was that cock fucking my ass.

'Go on then, Fuck Me! Stop playing around, rape my fuckin ass.'

That was me, crying, moaning, yelling, yet begging for more. Right then I wanted more. I needed to feel more as he shot his boiling streams of man juice up and inside my sorely abused hole. I needed abuse elsewhere to spread the pain, and I got it. As my fucker raised his body from mine someone else was laying across my shoulders and back with a belt.

'Yes! Yes! Yes!'

That was me again. I felt a rampant cock pushing at my gasping mouth and opened my lips and teeth to accept it, accept and worship it. Still the belt fell across my unprotected body, now my ass and back encouraging me to service that cock harder and deeper. I wanted that cock to fuck my mouth and throat as thoroughly as my ass had just been used. It did. I needed oxygen, my ass, back and hole were in agony, but still I never even grazed that cock with my teeth. I knew, somehow, who it belonged to, who was feeding me, who I wanted to take me.

In the second that sensation blasted into my brain the cock blasted down my throat, I reacted by diving deeper. My nose squashed against his groin, my lips tightened around the base of his shaft and I suckled and licked as best I could. I would have swallowed his cock, right down if that had been an option. I could feel myself going but just was unable to let go, my head was spinning. I needed to service that cock.

Next I found myself sitting over the edge of the truck, my head between my knees and gasping desperately for breath. A hand under my chin raised my head, I could see him more clearly now, his naked muscled body gleaming with sweat under the overhead lights. He had no concern about the audience, just about me. I could see it, I knew it. I knew he'd take care of me, as long as I deserved it, on his terms of course. There was no reason for me to say anything.

'He's mine,' I heard him say; 'I'm taking him home.' He had no concern for others opinions, this was what he wanted and this was what he would do.

'You can't have him; I'm selling him off down the park for a whipping.'

That was a voice I'd managed to half forget, the promise it had originally held out to me turned to disgust in my mind. I know he'd promised to hurt me and I agreed but had never expected the outcome in my wildest dreams.

'I've changed my mind,' I told him.

'You can't. I've got your clothes and bike. You won't get them back.'

'He won't need clothes this weekend,' retorted my rescuer, 'My dad will pick up the boys bike on his way home. Big Sarge wouldn't be happy if he knew what you really got up to over the state line would he.'

That seemed to be it, 'Go get in the back of that pickup,' he slapped my backside.

Hardly any comment from the audience to all this, they parted like the red sea, all those macho men, giving way to a lad in his early twenties leading his naked slave. Yes, I realized, that is what I'd just become. He helped me into the pickup with a swat across my ass, led me to the frame behind the cab and put my arms out to grab hold the top bar.

'Are you going to stand here boy or do I need to tie your hands?'

'I'll stand Sir.'

'Good boy. I'm taking you home to fuck, beat you, use you as my toilet and let you sleep at the foot of my bed. How's that sound to you?'

'Perfect Sir,' I replied.

A few moments later the pickup roared from the truck stop, his Masters naked slave standing proudly upright in the rear, exposed to the elements and any passing vehicles. His erect cock and tight balls were bouncing off the cab top, and he had a stupid smile stretching from side to side of his face. He'd finally found his Master and was going home.

—

– KARL'S BOY –

CHAPTER ONE

John never actually enjoyed abusing me quite as much as I got off on it myself. If truth be told I never admitted it to him but am sure he guessed that I knew. He had explained early on when our relationship turned sexual, inflicting a certain amount of pain was part of the humiliation I craved, and there was no way I could argue with that. He would never truly damage me but he did get some satisfaction seeing how much abuse he could inflict on my body. That's why we both so loved an audience, somehow it drove us to higher limits than the occasional times we played at home and also by some means he just knew when I had reached that final limit he shouldn't try to push me over, even though at times I was sure he had, and would tell him so in no uncertain terms, that he had gone too far.

It was really for our mutual enjoyment he would take me to a club every month or so. Oh! He never explained it that way, but then he never explained much of anything to do with sex after he first caught me experimenting on my own, just got on with it. But I guessed a visit might be on the way when he let me sleep unmolested for a couple of nights and so was not that surprised when he came in one Saturday, told me to clean myself up and then put on the clothes he would lay out on my bed.

I knew just what he expected and took a trip to the bathroom, starting with a warm enema followed by a thorough shower. When my body was soaking I turned off the water and rang the bell he had left on the shower shelf and turned to face the wall. I heard him enter soon after and felt the familiar shook as he sprayed my entire back, ass and legs with shaving foam. It didn't take him long these days to make sure my rear was free of body hair and he left without saying a word. Now it was my turn to do the same to my front, paying particular attention to my cock and balls. A quick face shave and then a second enema, this one always more uncomfortable. A second shower, this time allowed to use a shower gel, he said to make me smell nice but I had realized, also to help display a clean smooth skin for the intended audience.

Then down to my basement bedroom to see what he had decided I should wear. Tonight it was the usual full suspension body harness with a three-ring cock and ball cage over a tight rubber sheath with a piss exit. No underwear, a pair of short tight torn off denims. If the cock and ball cage hadn't held my cock straight up my stomach it would have fallen out the bottom. No socks, an old pair of short black leather boots and leather wrist and ankle straps completed the ensemble with a thick leather collar padlocked round my neck.

I dressed quickly and went back upstairs to find him already waiting. It was a warm night and he'd left his jacket off. Under his black T-shirt I could see the outline of his upper body harness. The bottom half was covered by combat trousers and lace-up black boots. He held a packed sports bag in one hand and held out the keys to my jeep four-track with the other, then turned, opened the front door and walked out, leaving me to set the alarm and lockup.

He was standing beside the passenger door, waiting for me to let him in, as I did, without word from either of us. I had hoped he would offer me a jacket or even a T-shirt to cover my upper body but all he said was 'We'll go to the Trock. Not been there for several months.'

This meant I had to drive halfway across town with just a leather harness as visible clothing. It may have been a warm night and we did sit higher than most cars, but even so I received more than a few curious looks from pedestrians and other occasional vehicles we passed on the way over.

When we got to the Trock I was lucky in being able to park in the next street. I still had to walk behind him to the club passing the gauntlet of several groups of pedestrians. Even in an area like this I made a somewhat unusual site on the open street. Once inside he told me to remove my shorts and hand them to the check out, and then walked me to the toilet. This was of a rather unusual design in having both a wide trough and a row of waist high urinals. He told me to sit between 2 of the bowls and having pulled my arms up to fastened off on some chains hanging for just such use, told me to behave myself and went off to the bar.

As you can probably guess this club catered to just his type of scene, and admittedly mine as well.

I looked around and saw the only other person in the toilet was about my age also dressed rather like myself though without the straps and crouching in front of the trough on the other side of the room. Wimp I thought to myself. There was no way John would let me crouch in front like that. Probably he would have me over there later and I knew if so I would be in a different position, troughs were for sitting in!

Over the next fifteen minutes or so over a dozen people entered the toilets, took care of immediate problems and in many cases remained to watch others do likewise. Being the type of cliental you would expect in a club like this none seemed particularly bothered seeing either of us in our respective positions and happily used one or the other as a receptacle for their excess liquid. There was some satisfaction in being aware I got more use than my companion. I knew better than to spill a drop at this time of night, when I got dirty John liked to oversee it himself. Sure enough he returned shortly holding a couple of cans of beer and quickly unshackled me.

'Has my boy been good?' he asked the audience.

Receiving affirmatives he turned to me. 'Need a piss?' I nodded. 'OK. Use him,' pointing to the other lad.

I quickly did as instructed, gratefully as I was feeling the pressure build up down below. He wasn't very good at swallowing my contribution and at least half spilled and flowed down his body. Twerp! I thought to myself. If you want to get washed all over you should lay down in the trough properly, where I half expected to be placed later on.

'Right then. That's the last time. Any more you hold until I say so,' was John's last instruction to me for some time.

I followed him to the bar where he chatted to some friends whilst I sat on the floor between his feet. He had several more beers, handing me one each time that I knew had to be drunk down quickly and of course after a little while I could feel that slight pressure building up again, nothing too important yet, just the knowledge a load was building up and would need release soon. John must have thought the same as he got off his bar stool and grabbing two more cans motioned for me to follow him to the rear of the bar.

The room was L shaped and the rear proper out of sight of the bar whilst still being the larger section of the room. This area was well furnished to appeal to people of our particular inclinations. The floor was solid tiles, which continued about a foot up the wall. There was a drain in one corner so the floor could be washed down but they never seemed to make much of an effort to do so. Hanging from the ceiling were a variety of chains and straps and dotted around were several oil drums both upright and on their sides. Also an old bath, a solid heavy kitchen table and a few chairs. The lighting, apart from a couple of pin spots, was dim and it could sometimes be difficult to see much through the smoke and heaving bodies.

There were probably around 20 people already there; some playing to a small degree, but even so the room was in no way crowded before we walked in, but as we were followed by what seemed like most of the bar, obviously some of them remembering out last visit and expecting to enjoy a repeat performance, the overall smell of male sweat and hormones and poppers thickened considerably as did the air of expectation. They intended to enjoy the performance, even if I didn't. Nobody was wearing much more than John and most much less, several wearing leather collars like mine, though I'd be surprised if any got used as I knew John intended to use me. Ages ranging all over the place, no real chickens, but quite late teens to sixties I thought with assorted bodies to match. Some trim and buffed and others large and sweaty even this early in the evening. It didn't seem as if much serious play had been occurring so far. That situation I knew quite well was about to change and was real glad when he handed me a bottle of poppers. 'You'll need that,' he said, loud enough for most of the room to hear.

'Anyone wants to examine my boy before I start on him?' he asked the room.

Damn stupid question. Of course they did and I nearly got knocked over in the rush as immediately there were hands over my body, fingers in my mouth, not always clean ones, twisting my nipples, pulling on my balls and getting more adventurous and abusive as John did nothing to stop them and I only buckled slightly under their abuse.

There were several hands round my backside, either slapping at it or in a couple of case attempting to finger fuck me. 'If you want to get in there you better bend him over,' came from John as he pulled me over to the table and forced me to lie over it at one end. It was just the right size and height to have me bent at the waist with my head reaching to the other side.

''Right then. Boy needs his ass examined fully. Anyone interested in the job?'

He must have pointed someone out because I heard someone gob and then spit in my ass crack followed by first two, then three and quickly four fingers. I couldn't help but moan at that, so would you with most of a hand stuck up inside of your ass without warning, feeling round to see how much they could hurt you. That still wasn't enough for him as I felt his hand removed and wiped over my back as he called out 'Can I use this metal plug then?'

John got back in the act then, 'Better get him spread fully if you intend to rape my boy with that?' and he kicked at my ankles, ''Spread your feet wide boy.'

As I obeyed he knelt down and clipped my ankles to rings on the table legs leaving my ass spread wide open for all. As I expected he then walked round the front and grabbed my wrists to attach likewise to rings on the other corners of the table, taking the poppers from my hand he held the bottle to my nose and told the others, 'All yours now.'

That was it I knew. He'd decided to go the whole hog. I wasn't going to be in for an easy night and he would love every moment of it.

Bastard!

CHAPTER TWO

I felt the application of a quick squirt of cold lube up my hole and then an even colder plug was forced slightly through my ass lips. I had seen from the corner of my eye what they intended to use on me, a six inch solid metal plug that opened out twice to a breadth you'd never get the fingers of one hand round and then back down to a very narrow shaft on a small oval plate. What I'd not been ready for was how cold it felt or how quickly it was forced in my ass to the first stop.

For the brief moment the plug had been in my view I'd seen it was one with two sections so there was still another stop to go. My hole had not been violated for a couple of days and so there had been time for it to recover somewhat, not to mention the plug was not only very cold but also very solid. I couldn't help it but gasp out a couple of swear words.

'Who told you to make any noise?' someone asked, 'Here comes the rest!'

That time I yelped and my body spasmed on the table. 'Can't have him thrashing around. Someone strap his body down.'

While one pair of hands played with my strapped cock and balls and another was twisting and turning the plug to get fuller deep access some others passed and fastened a pair of straps across my back and waist leaving me tightly fastened to the table at a right angle, my legs still just on the floor, my cock and balls dangling free, my ass available to one and all and my head just falling over the far edge.

'Can I really hurt him?'

'Of course you can, that's why I brought him here tonight just no blood and no perm damage,' replied John's voice as he placed the poppers back under my nose. I heard the unmistakable sound of a buckle being undone just by my ear followed by that of a belt being drawn through waist hoops. 'Here you are. Use this.'

'You fuckin' bastard!' I thought I'd said under my breath but John heard me.

'Definitely. If you think you can call me names like that, think again, I'm going to make sure you get real hurt and used tonight boy.' came his quick response.

At some signal the hands that had been running over my body, slapping at my ass and pulling on my balls were all removed and someone swung John's belt down across my backside with considerable force.

Crack!

It hurt. I yelled.

Crack! And again, Crack!

My ass stung and my joints popped as I tried unsuccessfully to pull my body away against the straps. Tears were already rolling down my face to the delight of some pervert close enough to lick them from my cheeks as they fell.

'Hey! Keep the noise down a bit will you. They'll hear it in the street.' There was a pause. 'Hmm! Nice red ass. Pity I'm on the door tonight. Stick something in his mouth will you. Just keep it down a bit.'

I'd stick this in,' came another voice, 'problem is I've seen his teeth snap when he gets belted and I don't fancy being castrated right now thanks.'

That's curable,' came John's voice, 'open wide boy.'

I opened my mouth wide to John's fingers but when I attempted to suck on them he pulled out and slapped my face, first one side and then the other.

'I just said to open wide. Not to enjoy yourself.'

He forced a rubber-coated ring into my mouth fastening the straps off behind my head. I'd not seen him bring that with him. It meant I was unable to close my mouth, whatever the circumstance.

'There you are. No clashing teeth. Mouth all yours.'

'That should do it,' said the earlier voice. 'You can carry on now and have fun. This should cool him down a bit.'

And I shivered as some cold wet fizzing liquid was slowly poured over my back, then my inflamed ass, running down my crack and over what part of my balls were not covered by the piss sheath.

'Open your eyes boy and see what your mouth is going to pleasure.'

A hand grabbed hold of my hair and pulled my head up slightly where I could focus on a semi erect jet-black uncut cock. Not too broad but it made up for that in length. Had to be an easy six inches and that was just semi erect.

He pushed the tip through my gag ring but when I went to lick it for him I received another slap across my face and the hand pulled my head up harder. If he kept on like that I'd be bald before morning.

'I didn't say you could enjoy yourself with my cock boy. I enjoy, you suffer, and that's how it goes.'

He must have given a signal as the belt was applied across my backside again.

Whack! Whack! Whack! No poppers this time.

I would have screamed if my mouth hadn't been blocked. It hurt like hell and there was no way I could even move my body to try and escape. His cock had hardened as he saw the strokes land and thrust itself straight down my throat without even giving me a chance to gag, but I sure knew it was there now. My eyes were streaming as I heard him speak out.

'Oh this is good good. I could feel him trying to yell. I do love a boy in pain. Someone else have a go at his ass.'

He grabbed hold of my hair again to raise my head as far as it would go and as he started to run his cock in and out through my lips and the rubber ring his other hand was slapping my face from time to time causing the hand holding my hair to pull even harder as my head swung from side to side.

Someone, probably John, stuck the poppers momentarily under my nose for which I was grateful as after being christened again with someone's drink my backside was being slapped by a series of hands, some softly and some hard as possible. My ass cheeks and my face cheeks hurt and my bladder was filling causing another pain as the stiff black cock filling my mouth and throat seemed to grow once again and my abuser started to rape my face with a vengeance. He had no mercy on me, he wanted to hurt me while he got the chance and was making sure he did a good job.

Every time he thrust deep down my throat, his thick crinkled groin hairs bashing my nose and his balls swinging under my chin he would pull my hair or slap my face and tell call out to the others.

, 'Slap him harder! Make him hurt so I can feel it down his throat. Don't play with him Hurt him! Make him feel it.'

Every slap either seemed to land where the belt had damaged me earlier or on the end of the solid butt plug causing that to jerk around inside my ass. The fact that a weight had now been attached to my bouncing balls was just another area of pain to endure as he let go of my hair and grabbing my head in both hands yelled out 'Yes! Yes!' and started to shoot jet after jet of boiling cum down my throat.

Finally his thrusting slowed and he partially withdrew his still half hard cock from my mouth.

'Now you can use your tongue to clean me up boy.'

'Can I piss in here as well?' I heard him ask.

'Be quick. Boy needs a bath before I let the crowd at him,' was John's reply.

It didn't take him long before, at first a few drops, shortly followed by a constant stream of hot acrid piss following his cum down my throat and this time causing me to gag on the volume but all he did was jam his groin back up to my mouth meaning I had to swallow or choke and making me fear slightly for my breath before his flow slowed and he pulled out finishing off by spraying my face and hair.

'Thanks Boss,' I could hear him say to John as the clips restraining my wrists and ankles were removed, as were the straps across my body and hands pulled me to my feet. 'I love to get a chance at his other end sometime,' he continued, 'Somewhere it wouldn't matter if he screamed.'

'Maybe later if you're still around,' John replied, ' I like to see a man who enjoys his play but right now I think he needs to wash down.'

That was when I realized my back and hair were covered in streams of quickly drying cum I'd never even felt land on my body during the earlier abuse. My backside felt hot and sore as did my throat when John removed the ring gag from my mouth. 'Get over there and take a bath before I have you strung up properly for these others to enjoy.'

Over there was only a few feet away, an old bath I'd vaguely been aware of people pissing in for some time. I was half walked, half led over. The time my body had been abused must have been longer than I'd realized as even in the poor light I could see a good few inches of mixed piss with streams of cum floating on the top.

'Go on. Get in,' accompanied by a slap on my still sore ass from John. 'Get in and let them see just what a filthy boy I own.'

CHAPTER THREE

I knew that there was no choice so slipped of my old boots and stepped over the edge to stand in sufficient piss and whatever to rise over my ankles. Someone had been busy. As my ass stretched in the process the metal plug fell out and clanged against the side of the bath. Worse for me in the immediate moment was the weight hanging from my balls that I'd managed to forget about with all the other abuse my body was attempting to recover from.

That weight caught against the bath side and jerked my squashed and already stretched ball sac, causing me to yelp. I grabbed my balls in a vain attempt to mitigate the pain only to have my hand slapped away and told to sit down. When I held back for a moment my balls were slapped again sending a sharp streak of pain shooting through my groin and told 'Sit down, or else!'

I knew when John sounded like that I had better do as instructed and carefully eased my body down till my legs and groin were almost covered by the cold stinking mess and my back rested for a moment against the end. For a second I could try to forget that John hadn't finished with me as my poor body tried to relax but that was not to be.

'I didn't tell you to lay down boy. Kneel up and wash yourself, thoroughly.'

Knowing better than to disobey I did as instructed and adjusted my body so that I knelt in the mess, my open asshole under water periodically burping as the wind escaped and causing the audience to laugh at me. I knelt my head forward till the top was under the liquid, using my hands to scoop up handfuls to soak those parts of my body still dry. I could feel from the slime that part of the contents were cum and probably spit but had no choice. If I didn't obey John wouldn't let me have my own rocks off later.

The audience helped out, adding fresh streams of piss from time to time, which they enjoyed aiming directly at my face and open mouth. Finally John said, 'That's enough fun for now. Get out.'

I stood up carefully, this time being much more aware of the ball weights as the straps were pinching tighter, aggravated by the cool piss and stuff running all over my body and dripping down from my hair. John must have seen me shiver as 'I'm sure this lot will soon get you warmed up boy,' was his only comment he led me over to the middle of the room where a couple of pin spots shone on an area framed by two scaffolding poles fastened floor to ceiling about four foot apart.

I knew this was what he'd been looking forward to all evening. My whole body available for total abuse, while he watched. Standing me between the poles I spread my legs ready for him to fasten off my ankle straps at the bottom of the poles. Then he asked for assistance as my arms were raised and fastened off higher up leaving my body slightly stretched, spread-eagled, easily accessible and trapped.

'Where's that plug,' John asked, and after someone handed it to him as he came up behind me and clutching my body to his with one arm round my chest used the other to ram the solid metal plug straight back up my hole knowing he was inflicting more pain and causing me to yell out a response.

'What's that you said boy?' he asked.

'It hurt Sir,' was my reply.

What did you expect? That's what I've brought you here for. So I can watch people hurt you boy. I enjoy that and so will you if you want to please me.'

'Please sir, no sir.'

How much did I mean it? Suddenly I wasn't quite so sure. Yes, I got off on being hurt and other abuse and John liked to watch it happen it as well and that was all right by me, but it still hurt. But then, occasionally, very occasionally, I really got off myself to a different level by being hurt and abused, usually with an audience of strangers watching and getting involved but knowing somewhere in the back of my mind that John was also there. Was this going to be one of those occasions? Some inner being told me it could be and that thought helped buoy me up for what came next.

My body hurt everywhere it seemed. Ass inside and out, stretched mouth and sore throat, sides of my face, stretched balls and now I was standing with a painfully filling bladder. In the seconds it took for that thought to flash through my mind John had attached a tube from the rubber sheath over my cock and I knew he'd taken it round my back and plugged the other end into the metal plug shoved up my ass which was now held in place with a leather strap. When I finally had to let it go I would be pissing up my own ass.

Then John moved back, 'Right then. He's all yours for a bit. Just make sure he don't dry out inside or out,' that with a little laugh, adding 'just keep my boy fed with poppers.'

That did it. Well what else you would expect in an extreme leather club where the average customer could only fantasize about the type of sex they wanted and then a 19-year-old lad with a decent bronzed body from regular outdoor exercise every day suddenly became available, it was absolute chaos.

It seemed every inch of my stretched spread-eagled body was covered by hands and fingers, touching, pinching, slapping, pulling and twisting, much harder and intrusively than before Bottles were poured into my mouth from time to time when they could get past the fingers trying to fuck my face, some containing beer and some other substances, much of which ran down my face to join the liquid

61

streaming still from my hair as my earlier bath was being continued by a couple of helpers pouring fresh filled bottles over my head.

I seemed to be on fire everywhere, each nipple had a different pair of teeth working on it, the hands slapping at my backside were getting bolder and though my body couldn't move much each slight swing as they attacked it caused the weights on my balls to swing back and forth increasing the pressure there even more. I could hear voice talking to me, asking me questions but I just was unable to understand them. I couldn't concentrate. Finally I felt the pressure on my bladder give way and within seconds a hot flush filled my bowels.

I knew what had happened but really just didn't care anymore. Let them see me piss myself full. They'd seen everything else. I wanted them to use me, to abuse me, to enjoy hurting me, just to enjoy themselves. All of them. In fact I just couldn't be bothered any longer. I was starting to fly and my body was a separate issue.

Someone was slapping my face and talking to me. Why? Why did I have to talk? Couldn't they just get on with it and leave me alone?

Somehow or other he got through to me, it was John. 'You've just pissed yourself. You need to be punished. OK?'

Of course it was OK. I was strung up here to be punished. John liked to punish me, even at times when I'd not done anything wrong. Even better he liked to see others hurt me. I liked to be punished didn't I? After all I was his boy tonight and here to be hurt. It was what I was for, I wanted to fly.

More face slapping. 'Do you need any more poppers or a gag?'

I just managed from somewhere to dredge up a vocal reply, ' That would be a waste.'

He hugged me tightly to him, 'Good boy,' and kissed me hard, shoving his tongue right inside my mouth and when we were running out of breath pulled back just far enough to spit on my face before calling out 'Carry on.'

Whack!

The belt landed across my ass, the small belt holding the plug in my hole not giving me much protection.

Whack!

That felt different somehow. Were they passing it around? I didn't care.

Whack!

A longer pause. Definitely passing the belt round. That one had really stung!

Whack! Whack!

Yes! That hurt! I loved it.

Whack!

My body swayed back and forth slightly from the force of the blows causing the balls weights to set up a rhythm I encouraged whenever I could.

Whack!

'Chickens!' I cried out. 'Don't you know how to use a boy properly?'

Whack!

That one was across my back. They were getting better but I was almost gone. My body remained there still for them to enjoy and to get pleasure from its reactions but I was off somewhere else. I'd worked out that this must be what some people felt like on hard drugs but my way had to be much better. This was my high, it didn't happen often but when it did I could stretch my wings and fly. With any luck the afterglow would last the whole weekend and the only serious after effects would be some bruising, and living with that could be a high of sorts all on its own

Whack! Whack!

Two in quick succession that time, back and front, ass and chest.

'Finally a real man to enjoy me! Go on you perves. Get your rocks off! Fly me!'

Well why not, I was flying anyway. I hardly knew what I was yelling but sure as hell I wasn't screaming out in pain. John would be proud.

Whack! Whack! Whack! Whack!

Back and forth the belt fell across my upper body, someone was really into it. I hardly noticed when it stopped, only that I was no longer holding myself upright but had sagged between the poles and only the straps at my wrists were stopping my body from crashing onto the floor. Had I passed out? Who cared? I sure didn't, just wanted it to carry on.

John was removing the straps and weights from my cock and balls, the pain when my circulation returned down there an excruciating delight and then, when the belt round my waist was removed allowing the solid metal plug blocking my hole to shoot out with a blast of wind and a stream of piss still hot from being caught inside my bowels, was matched there by a such a feeling of relief I felt like kissing everybody present.

'Do you still want to rape this hole before I take it away?' That was John, obviously offering the service of my body to someone as he finished by striping the cock sheaf and piss tube from my body. For the first time since we left home my cock and balls were free to the air and showed their gratitude by almost immediately springing to attention. A glorious, painful, erection.

'Hell Yes!'

Someone was accepting John's offer to violate my body.

CHAPTER FOUR

My ass was still leaking when my body was flung over one of the filthy oil drums lying on its side forcing the breath from my chest and slamming my very tender balls against the drum. Even though my brain had almost closed down it still hurt and my body objected and tried to get away.

'Someone hold his wrists. Don't want him thrashing around and this will give the boy something to complain about.'

My wrists were grasped as a hairy groin appeared just in front of my face. There was no time to inspect it however as a huge hot throbbing cock was shoved straight in and down my poor hole causing me to yell out again. The fact that my brain was prepared to accept almost anything done to my body didn't mean I couldn't feel it.

'Don't play with it you fucker! You're supposed to make me feel it!'

Any other observations I may have been about to make regarding the abuse of my hole were cut off with my breath as my abuser's hands found my nipples and pinching deeply started fucking my ass with a vengeance.

The oil drum was supposed to be laid in a cradle to hold it steady but the force of the battering my rear was receiving caused a slight roll back and forth which also placed my continually open mouth in line with the hard cock jutting out from the hairy groin in front of my face. With the pain in my rear and nipples building I didn't dare attempt to close my mouth to attend to it as the owner might have wished, I had enough trouble just keeping it open enough to breath.

Even so, as the cock seemed to realize my problem it moved forward allowing a couple of inches to lie on my tongue. Then the hands holding my wrists were replaced and a couple of fingers appeared either side of the cock wedging my mouth more fully open and as my wrists were pulled tighter the rocking of my body being rolled back and forth slowly forced the cock further and further in my mouth and started down my throat as it throbbed and swelled to take up almost all the available space.

I wanted to scream with pain, to yell at the bugger fucking my ass to do it harder, for someone to really hurt my, but I could hardly breathe sufficiently to remain conscious. I was choking on the cock now quite forcibly fucking my mouth. I had to switch at least some attention to my brain and that cock trying to fuck my brains out.

I could hear voices, 'Go on, fuck him harder! Spit roast him! Fill him, stiff him, hurt him. Don't play with him, that boy needs to be hurt!'

On and on, all round me. There were several other hands on my body, some just trying to restrict my thrashing and spreading the cum and spit landing from everywhere more evenly, and a couple I could feel squeezing and stretching my ass cheeks allowing my abuser to fuck me deeper.

My throat was suddenly fully blocked as the engorged cock trying to breed my mouth swelled even further and started pumping what felt like a gallon of hot cum straight down to my stomach and the attached hairy groin made a reasonable attempt to break my nose as it slammed forward. Luckily for me the cock was pulled back to my lips allowing me just time for a quick gasp before slamming back in and jetting another spurt of cum down my throat. Six or seven times that happened before being slowly withdrawn, followed by the fingers that were wiped off in my hair while the cock was slapped back and forth across my face.

The hands holding my wrists and head disappeared and my upper body collapsed over the drum, my hands touching the floor and the blood rushing to my head.

I was gasping, trying somehow to get some oxygen back in my body before I passed out, I'd almost lost feeling in my balls from the bashing they were getting but all my idiot brain could so was try and cry out, 'Rape me you fucking bastard!

Go on. Do me properly!'

He did. Fuck! Fuck! Deeper and deeper, harder and harder. My eyes were streaming tears but there was just no energy left to yell or cry out. I hurt everywhere but all I wanted was more. I wanted him to hurt me deeper, not just for John to watch and enjoy, not for the audience, now I wanted it for myself.. I wanted, needed, to be hurt and abused. I didn't care what they did as long as they hurt me.

Then it happened. I could feel his cock, as large and long as it was, throb and increase even more in size and as he pulled right out past the lip and then thrust back in, deeply, past all and any obstacles, he shot. A boiling jet of man juice burning me up. He didn't keep thrusting in and out but leaning over caught hold of my lank hair with one hand pulling my head up to a level where he could use his other hand to slap it from side to side. 'That's how a man fucks a boy toy,' he said, 'Forcibly and painfully.'

'Yes!' I yelled, 'Oh yes! That's what boy is for! To be enjoyed.'

Just then the lights flicked on and off several times warning us the club was closing and he gave no thought to my poor exhausted and abused body but pulled straight out without finesse our warning, just walking round to my front and pulling my head up again by its hair shoved his cock at my mouth, 'Clean it boy.'

As I did my best to lick and clean off the residue cum and slime on his cock from my ass it crossed my mind I'd not really seen any of the faces, or even much of the bodies that had used me tonight. Even as that thought crossed my mind however he pulled out and just dropped my head back down to hit the oil drum and I had no energy to lift it up on my own to look. I was so dead beat, I just couldn't move, or so I thought.

A couple of quick slaps across my sore backside from John's plastic ruler soon cured that idea. I'd not been aware he'd brought it with him and it always seemed unfair that a twelve inch piece of flexible plastic applied from a couple of inches could cause so much pain, quite different from that of his belt.

'Get up boy. You need a wash before we go on.'

Go on? Where? Hadn't I been used enough for him tonight? Of course not. He could tell I was flying and the longer he could keep that up the more fun we would both get. But there had to be a limit as to how much more my body could take, whatever my brain was telling me otherwise.

That flashed through my mind in a second even as I'd managed to get to my feet and walk over to the bath now quarter full of piss and cum and spit and only knows what else. The lights had come up and there were still a few people around to see what might happen and that was John saying, 'Get in boy and have a proper wash before we go.'

I went in. Boy had to do what John told him didn't he? Actually in some ways the vile cooling mixture was balm to my sorely abused body and I did as instructed, kneeling down, first fully dipping my head and face then making sure I washed well round and inside my ass.

When I stood up and got out John handed me a large glass of what I could smell was brandy and asked, 'Will you need anything else boy?'

'No Sir.' I replied to receive a big grin. John knew me too well.

'Follow me then boy.'

I followed him back into the bar, now fully lit due to imminent closure and my filthy soaking bruised naked body on full display to the few customers and staff remaining. He took the now empty glass from me and placing it on the bar asked the two barmen, 'Do you still want to use boy? You can have his face at any rate.'

'Oh Yes!'

'I'll take him up to the woods if you can get there in the next hour and let him have another large brandy now to keep his strength up.'

An Hour? How much more was in store? Goody Goody. I don't need to tell you the brandy was good as well.

'You know it was raining earlier. Be a bit muddy up there now.' They told him.

'You can put your boots back on,' looking down at my naked feet, then directing me to stand outside the toilets, just a few feet from the open door John collected his bag from reception.

'Stay there while I unlock the van and put a sheet down,' and went outside into the night leaving my naked body on view to anyone passing, also to the not so gentle attentions of the last remaining customers.

Looking over into the toilets I could see the piss lad from earlier was getting himself back together, having a wash down from the sink and slowly getting dressed. I doubt he had much use tonight.

John came back in and followed my gaze into the toilet. 'Follow me,' and grabbing the chain now attached to the collar round my neck he pulled me in and in stopped in front of one of the open seat less toilets.

'Kneel.'

I knew what he wanted and knelt down, my knees either side of the bowl and my head half inside. 'Do you want to piss?' I heard him ask the other lad. 'Well come over here and piss over my boys head then pull the flush. That's how a real boy should be used. Not just sit there and let someone piss in your mouth.'

Someone, probably the lad, did just as John had suggested and then pulled the flush, probably for the first time that night, which rinsed my hair OK as the liquid rose but also made me drink mouthfuls of dilute mixed piss to save from drowning.

John's hand grabbed on my neck chain and pulled me upright, piss and water once more streaming down my naked body.

'What's those marks on his body?' the lad asked.

Everybody's been enjoying my boy,' John replied. 'You've got a lot to learn yet I can see.'

'I shouldn't think I'd enjoy that. Does he?'

'Don't care if he enjoys or not. I do and that's all that matters.'

Back out by reception John continued, this time to me as he dropped my old boots at my feet, 'The trucks just down the street. Go and get in the back, I don't want your mess on the seats.'

'He's still naked,' I heard the lad exclaim.

'So what? I'm not getting my truck dirty for no reason and he will be even filthier before this night is over.'

'What do you mean?'

'He's going up to the woods to be used a bit more and I hear its muddy there tonight.'

'Can I come? Please.'

I'd never heard someone so childishly eager; probably he'd not had much experience, not been lucky enough to find a man like mine.

'Anyone can come. This boy is Open Season tonight. Want a lift? You can get in the back and amuse yourself with him on the way up.'

Was I being handed over to a novice? John better hang around to keep him in limits. What was I talking about? Limits? There didn't seem to be many of those concerning my body tonight, or rather, this morning, Then John handed the lead attached to my collar over to the lad, ' Here you are. You can take him down to the truck. Back doors are unlocked, boy knows which one, all you have to do is smack his bottom a couple of times and he will get in.'

I was torn in half a dozen directions. John letting others use my body was one thing but he'd never just handed me over like that before. Part of me wanted to object but I couldn't do that and anyway, that other part of my body being controlled by my stupid brain was getting off on being led dripping wet and naked down the street to John's truck. I knew it was a gay area but anyone could be about, straights came down to look sometimes, and after the pubs closed quite a few would come down for a sly blowjob on the side.

Even with my head bent down to watch where I placed my feet I heard enough comments to appreciate there were still quite a few people about of both persuasions as I was led along hoping to glimpse the back of John's truck but also proud of the marks on my body and my painful erection out in the open for all to see.

Catching a glimpse of John's truck from the corner of my eye I jerked my head in an attempt to tell my temporarily controller. How do you communicate with someone when you are not allowed to talk without permission and he has no way of understanding your signs?

Lucky me. I heard My Masters voice and saw the rear doors being opened. 'Here you are. I forgot to tell you boy is not allowed to talk unless I say so. Make him get in, he knows what to do.'

He may have been an almost novice compared to us but the slaps he gave my still burning backside didn't hold back and with a whimper I crawled inside, removed my boots and lay down on my stomach, squashing my cock and balls as carefully as possible under my groin and grabbing hold of the rings bolted in each far corner.

'It's not safe to tie him down when we're moving but Boy knows not to move now. Do you want to get in with him?'

It seemed two bodies clambered in the back and sat down on the padded wheel arches either side of my body. Then I felt my legs being tapped and opened them out toward the other rings John sometimes used to fasten me to when he took me cruising.

Both doors slammed so he was bringing at least one more person up with us and as he started the motor his voice came through to the back, 'OK. Do you think you can enjoy yourselves back there for the next fifteen minutes?'

CHAPTER FIVE

'What can I do to him?'

'Almost anything you want I guess,' came a reply from the other person in the back with us.

'Will your boy need holding down?' that obviously directed as John.

'Not tonight,' came the boastful reply from the cab.

It was true. I didn't need controlling any more in order to allow John to feel proud and enjoy himself. Tonight I was flying from the misuse my body had suffered and the endorphins that abuse had released were speeding through my body. It made me proud to be thought of as John's boy and was prepared now to suffer on his behalf.

Hands lightly felt at my wounded back and ass causing me to groan at which point they were rapidly withdrawn. 'That's all right. Boys allowed to make noises when someone uses him. That's how you know he's hurting.' John just wouldn't stop talking.

'Can he turn over?'

'Of course, 'just don't bring him off.' There was John again.

I turned and I lay back, spread-eagling my arms to grasp hold of the rings and then spread my feet the same way, just as I knew I should.

'Can I?' I heard.

There must have been a nod and next I felt a hand slapping very lightly at my cock. It was quite bruised and so I let out a little whimper but there was no way he was going to make me cry playing with it like that. The other occupant in with us had the same idea as I felt the van sway as they moved down between my legs and sat or knelt grasping my ankles in his hands.

'Go on then. Do it like you mean it. He isn't going to move.'

'Won't it hurt him? Won't he mind?'

'No matter if he minds and of course it will hurt him,' came the reply, 'That's what he's for.'

That was enough. No more tender love taps. He started slapping my cock back and forth, up and down, causing somewhat more than just a whimper or so to escape.

'Look at his face. Its best when you can see the pain in their eyes but the mouth is a pretty good guide as well.' I was gritting my teeth in a vain attempt not to offer too vocal a response to his ministrations but not doing so very well.

Then a hand clutched at my balls pulling them slightly downwards leaving my cock stuck at forty-five degrees. 'Now give his cock another work out. You should see his Master use a belt on it. That really makes him squeal.'

He'd seen me used before then. I had no chance to try and place his voice as the other hand returned to its abuse, only this time, with my cock being too stretched to fly around his slaps were really hurting, drawing yelps from me at each slap. I heard a giggle and the hand increased its speed, back and forth, back and forth.

'Could I make him scream?' he asked.

'You can try and make him yell if you like when we get into the woods,' came from John in the front. 'Better give him a bit of a rest now so he's fresh when we get there.'

Fresh? There was no way I'd be fresh in a hurry, I knew I'd need at least a week to recuperate from tonight, even so, a slight intermission as it were would not come amiss.

'How much longer to the woods?' he asked.

'About another five minutes.'

'Damn. I need to piss again badly.'

'Use his mouth then. It's what he's got it for.'

'Do you mean he swallows?'

'Of course,' said John, 'Don't you?'

Not much if I can help it,' he replied. Christ. No wonder he didn't get much use in the toilet. Come to think of it, when I pissed in his mouth earlier he hadn't really swallowed, just crouched there with his mouth open for it to flow in and out. He had a lot to learn. Must be why John had invited him, he'd probably get off on using me to instruct some young newbie.

He clambered up to sit astride my body. 'Scoot right up, pull his head onto your cock and then jam it between your thighs. I felt his bare legs either side of my chest and then a naked groin at my face with what I guessed was a five inch uncut cock place carefully in my mouth where I gripped it with my lips. He must have slipped his shorts off.

'Now reach behind and grab hold of his nipples, you can play with them while you piss.'

'Won't he bite?'

'My Boy never bites,' came from John, 'Just don't try and tear his nipples off.'

Oh hell. Here we go again. I felt his naked thighs grip tighter and contract as he pinched at my nipples causing my body to flex and he started to empty his bladder. He may not have been swallowing earlier but must have been drinking something as the fact he'd emptied himself over my head some ten minutes ago seemed to have made no difference to the dilute flow that gushed from his cock and down my throat now.

It was a good thing my throat had been opened up earlier otherwise I'd probably have had a problem swallowing the flood, as it was there was a slight leakage from the side of my mouth onto the rubber sheet John had laid out on the van floor. As the flow slowed I felt his cock start to harden and letting go of my nipples he relaxed his thighs and grabbed hold of my head jerking it up and down to use as a wanking machine.

'Don't waste it,' I heard, I'm parking up now and you can have his ass later if you like.'

'Yes please,' he gasped out, 'It's OK, I usually want to come twice in a short period.'

Oh bugger!

As I felt the van draw to a stop he continued to fuck my face and never even slowed down when the back doors were opened turning the interior light on. If his hands had not been holding my head from behind I'd probably have been knocked unconscious the way he was jerking it up and down, his own fingers must have been bruised but that didn't in any way seem to deter him. Slam! Swallow! Choke! Again and again! This was no sub, more like a bad master in the making and, it would seem, one who's enjoy inflicting pain just because he could.

'God I hope I get to fuck you later boy. Make you really yell. I'd get off on that.'

He was getting off just talking about it I could tell from the way he was forcing my head into his groin and his now jerking cock but there was no way he'd make me yell with a cock that size up my ass, very nice cock though it was.

It was almost as if he'd heard my thoughts, 'I'll get someone to thrash your stomach while I fuck you and I'll be able to watch you scream at the same time. Oh Yes!'

With that he shot a load of cum deep down my throat to join the previous deposits I received that night. One stupid part of me thought I'd have to go on a diet after all the protein I'd been fed of late, while another part became apprehensive about his promise. There was no time to reflect on that as the moment he finished shooting it was just a quick withdrawal, wiped his cock down with his hand and that over my face, then jumped back out from the van to a round of applause.

As I slowly sat up and looked out I caught a glimpse of him pulling his shorts back on and a group of about ten others crowded round the door where they had obviously been enjoying his performance, and the view of my laid out naked body thrashing around beneath him.

John told me to leave my boots and get out and as I stood outside in full view told me to 'Kneel,' and refastened the lead to my collar when I did so. I had heard correctly before, the earlier rain had cleared leaving a clear sultry night but also a layer of mud here in the parking area.

'Here you are,' I heard from him and looked up wondering what he meant only to see him pass the lead to the lad who's just been fucking my face. This wasn't right. He was no older than myself and had no idea how a boy like me should be treated. Then John also passed him his shoulder bag, 'You may find a use for some of this,' and as the lad looked in he smiled in a strange way. 'Thanks. Are there any limits?' Maybe he did have an idea even if previously only in his fantasies.

'Just nothing broken, no blood or blisters and Boy must be able to take me on when we get home. Anything you're not sure about check with me, I'll be around somewhere.'

Shit! Shit! Shit!

CHAPTER SIX

The almost evil grin on his face should have warned me when he jerked hard on my leash and pulled me away from the vehicles into the middle of the car park where my naked body was in full view of all and sundry. This was not a one hundred percent gay meeting place at night, usually gay to my right, straight to my left and any other mix in the middle. This wasn't the club where every participant or otherwise, everyone knew the scene. The voices I could make out confirmed my fears, male and female, shock, horror, laughs, encouragement to my controller, but no sound I could hear of engines starting and people rushing away in disgust.

Cars were parked all round the edges of the park where shadow and trees gave some camouflage but out here in middle where the ground dipped slightly retaining an obvious pool of mud we were in full and uninterrupted view, helped considerably by an almost full moon.

He walked me into the deepest part of mud pool where my feet were half covered and then reached into John's bag and removed a connected set of clamps which he reached over and attached painfully to my tender nipples. I was right; he did seem to know what everything was for. It just remained to be seen if he was experienced enough to use them, and me, properly. Next he brought out a metal

78

weight on a eighteen inch chain and motioning me forward clipped it to the strap round my cock and balls allowing the weight to fall from his hand and jerk horribly on my balls.

'Go and stand in the mud, open your legs and then don't move! Don't dare move. Get your head up so people can see your face better. Don't say a thing, nothing at all. I don't care how much you yell or scream or moan. Got it?' With that last he slapped my face a couple of times and I almost answered before just turning it into a grunt and nodding my head. 'Good.'

Raising my head whilst slowly shuffling back I got a better look at his body than had been possible before. Just wearing some loose dirty cotton shorts and trainers I could see a nicely buffed olive skinned body his early twenties with no body hair to be seen apart from quite thick dark curls on his head. He had John's bag of tricks on his shoulder and delving in pulled out his belt and his cat. 'One now and one later. Your choice.' He held them both toward me, one in each fist, also making sure our audience could see what he held even if too far away to hear.

John's belt was a two inch wide well used three foot length of flexible leather and his cat was made up from twenty; two foot lengths of one eighth inch rubber with the top third bound round into a handle. I knew exactly how that was made as John had allowed me to design and assemble it under his directions and there were several earlier variations he'd considered didn't hurt me enough when he experimented with them on my body.

I also knew from experience the cat after my ass had been belted red could actually cause short term damage and so nodded at the cat, it only half crossing my mind at that moment what a crazy situation this was. Not only were my feet standing a couple of feet apart in a muddy puddle with a heavy weight hanging from my balls, the only articles I was wearing that could be considered clothing were a few leather straps and my harness, standing all around were a group of people most of whom had never seen anything like it before but knew now I was about to be whipped and I had just responded as if it were the most natural thing in the world that I would be asked what implement would be used to inflict pain on my body.

79

Somehow, natural or not, it was right. John had lent me out to this lad who wanted to hurt and humiliate me in public and that was John's choice. Just the sight of those implements had anyway sent me half way back to where my body had been in the club. I was astonished at how easy it seemed to separate my mind and look at myself from another perspective. Someone else watched the lad walk round my body and out of sight, someone else felt the lash of John's cat land across his back and whilst the body swayed little sound escaped through the clenched teeth.

Even so, a body has to breath from time to time and at the third lash, which landed over my buttocks, I discovered myself moaning as my body swayed back and forth from the assault also causing the weight hanging from my balls to swing at its own rate.

'Don't just watch from back there. Why not come closer and watch him really get used? Don't be shy.'

'Don't it hurt him?' I heard a female voice ask.

'Of course,' that came from my abuser, 'that what I enjoy. He'll be hurt a lot more before this nights finished.'

'But what about him? How can he enjoy it?' came that female voice again, from somewhere behind me.

'Who said he had to enjoy it?'

Opening my eyes I discovered quite a few male bodies of varying descriptions standing within view, several with female company. All of them appeared to be looking at my cock with its swinging weight apart from the one with the girl who was staring intently at my face.

'Go on! Whip him again,' I heard someone say, and strokes landed back and front, shoulders paired with chest, lower back with stomach, ass paired with groin. I yelled. He'd pulled back slightly on the stroke but even so the throngs landing on and wrapping round my tender cock and balls were excruciating sending a sharp pain right through my groin and causing my body to almost double up and loose balance. I just managed to steady my body but to my horror felt a blast of wind escape from my backside, realizing the same time my bladder was also requiring release.

'That's disgusting,' came from the irritating female behind me. It was, I could also feel some liquid escape from my bowels running down my leg but had no idea what it was.

You'd be the same if your ass had been raped like his tonight.

'Is he gay then?'.

Do it matter? His ass and mouth available for anything that comes out of a cock? Anybody want him?'

'Go on Karl,' from that whiney female behind me, 'You know we can't tonight, it's the wrong time. Let's see you do his face, there's nothing gay about that.'

'Can I really?' asked a young rough male voice, 'I'm randy enough to fuck anything tonight but I ain't gay.'

'That's OK. You don't need to be gay to fuck a mouth.'

'How do I get him to do it?' asked the same rough voice as a young bother boy walked round in front of me. He was about five foot ten or eleven, well built in a lean way though I could see him thickening out in a few years but right now his body was in peak perfection in dirty, torn tight jeans with a leather biker's jacket and body hugging oil marked tee undershirt. I was torn between looking at the bulge his hands were rubbing in his jeans and his face where startling white teeth showed in a dark sun bronzed face and the tip of a pink tongue just pushing through.

He may never have used a man before but I could see the idea was getting him off.

'Just tell him what you want; how you want him, then it's up to you. Fuck his mouth or piss in it, whatever turns you on. He's yours'

John had already passed me over to this lad for a session and now the lad was passing me around to all and sundry in turn as if it the most natural thing in the world.

'Come here and kneel,' said the dirty teen as he unzipped his fly.

I moved forward slightly and knelt down at the edge of the mud pool a few inches from a short fat circumcised cock. I could feel the heat escaping from his groin and the smell stale piss and motor oil among other things.

He thrust his groin forward reaching my lips with his smelly cock that was already starting to rise to its full operating size and position, about seven inches but being well compensated for any possible shortcomings there by its breadth.

'You nick it with your teeth and I'll knock your fuckin' head off,' accompanied by a slap to my head that nearly bowled me over.

Opening my mouth as wide as possible I inched forward slowly allowing him to enter my mouth, attempting to wash his cock with my tongue on the way. I was right, his cock was dirty, stale piss, sweat, smeg, it was all I could do not to retch and I felt him stumble, but then he grabbed hold either side of my head by my hair to steady himself.

'Fuck boy! She won't even put her mouth on it, says it's too big, let alone wash it like that. You're better than a hand job already.'

Those words and the feel of his hands grabbing my hair were all it took to pull my chain and I decided to give him a blow job to remember though somehow, given the present situation, I thought it unlikely he'd be forgetting it in a hurry anyway. As my mouth slowly swallowed his cock I found it more and more difficult to wash due to the lack of space for my tongue to operate and so concentrated on tightening my lips and slowly moving my head just slightly back and forth. Judging by the trembling I could feel through his cock from his body he was really getting into it now and I risked raising my hands behind him to his buttocks and pulling him suddenly forward, my nose jamming into his sweaty smelly groin and his cock almost choking me, then pulling my head back against his hands in my hair so just the first inch of his cock lay on my teeth.

'I ain't fuckin gay! Get your hands off my ass!'

82

I merely grabbed his cheeks through the denim again and pulled his cock rapidly through my tight lips, and then pulling against his hands once more pulled back, this time taking a risk to slightly massage his ass cheeks.

He didn't complain that time, or the next couple of thrusts I encouraged. Then when his cock was lying just that inch in my mouth I slacken my lips and grabbing tighter at his ass also used my teeth to nibble on his cock. He pulled right out and letting go of my hair slapped me round the side of my head causing my body to overbalance and fall to one side in the mud pool. Half expecting something of the sort I was able to resume my earlier position almost at once, my hands down by my side and looking up at his face.

'You like that then? You want me to hit you? Hell what are you? Stupid?'

'He's my boy and he's here to be used and abused. Of course you can hit him, whatever you like, just nothing broken and no blood. I need his body available later for myself.' That was John. He was watching and enjoying. I smiled.

'What are you smiling at boy?' asked the boy, 'Come here, I'll give you something to stop you smiling.'

He undid his belt pulling it through the hoops of his jeans, I noticed his lack of underwear, allowing them to fall to the ground and with one hand holding his belt used the other to grab my hair and twist pull my head so my mouth lay under his almost hairless dangling balls. 'Clean them if you know what's good for you.'

Of course I knew what was good for me but did as instructed anyway. Like his cock they were rank with stale sweat and piss but as the taste of his cock was still in my mouth managed to swab them down without too much difficulty, even taking each one into my mouth and pulling down sufficiently to make him wheeze. I could feel his continually erect cock slapping against my forehead from time to time so it was obviously working well for him as well.

As I let his second ball sac escape my mouth he pulled away again and used his hand again to slap me across my face, back and forth. 'I said to clean, not suck. I can see why you deserve to be hurt, not doing what you're told. Now get back up here so I can fuck your face.'

Kneeling back up properly he fed his belt around my neck and pulled my head forward until my open mouth met and enveloped his now happily rampant cock. He just laid the first couple of inches inside my mouth and said, 'You won't be nibbling on me again will you?' and accompanied that question with a tightening pull of his belt around my neck. As I just allowed my lower teeth to rise and slide along the under shaft of his cock he continued, 'You know better than to nibble your food by now don't you?'

I brought my upper teeth down and spent a couple of moments very lightly seesawing my teeth back and forth, left and right while he held my hair in one hand and his belt in the other, slowly pulling it tighter round my neck. He was getting off on this - and so was I.

Finally the belt closing round my neck became too much and I had to pull off his cock.

Immediately he pushed his hand in my face and shoved me over on my back into the mud pool. 'Told you not to chew your food,' he said with a big grin. 'Naughty boys need to punished.'

Looking up I could see that at some time he'd managed to remove his jeans entirely, also his jacket and T and was just standing there, all five foot ten or eleven inches of what really seemed to be a fantastic young body in his socks and boots. Probably worked on a building site I thought as almost full tan apart from a section round his groin and even that had been allowed some exposure. Quite curly long black greasy hair on his head but very little on his well-defined body that was running with sweat. Straight or gay, he had no qualms about showing his body of in mixed company or in having his way with mine.

I lay back in the mud looking up that body as he walked forward to stand astride and lifting one dirty boot placed it on my stomach pressing down slightly. When I only looked back at him with a slight gasp his smile increased and placing that foot back beside me raised the other boot, staring now directly into my eyes.

I managed a very slight nod of acceptance and he brought it down between my thighs, pressing directly against my cock and balls.

'Hey wait for us,' I heard a shout somewhere in another life, 'We were promised a go with him as well.'

CHAPTER SEVEN

Heck! It was the club staff, I'd forgotten all about them. It wasn't that I was concerned as to their intentions. It wasn't for me to care anyway. Just as long as people kept on hurting and using me I couldn't say no anyway, could I? But there was something about this straight boy that was different and I wanted him to please keep on doing it me, hurting my body anyway.

I have no idea actually where 'me' had got to, somewhere else watching all this and getting high on the process. Hell! I was so far away it was far too much of an effort to try and listen to what was happening around my body but the belt round my neck was being used to make me sit up while the boot pressing on my balls was trying to squash them flat so I had to try and concentrate or be choked, and turned into a eunuch.

'Are we too late? Is it finished? Can we still have a go at him?'

'He's finished when I say,' that was John, 'This nice hetro lad's giving boy a good work out at the moment but you lot can be next.'

The boot attempting to flatten my cock and balls was removed causing my cock to swing up on my stomach in a half erect position and I just couldn't help it, my bladder finally let go with such force that even in my sitting position my face and gasping open mouth received a full blast which in turn caused a variety of comments from the mixed audience, mainly of disgust

To my surprise the lad who'd been fucking my face appeared quite unfazed with the situation.

'What's so gross about that? If we can fuck him and spit on him then piss ain't any different. He'll be getting another mouthful from me soon anyway.'

He lent down and grabbing hold of the belt he'd previously placed round my neck half dragged me away from the pool of mud. There was mud daubed all over, not only my back and legs but also splashed over my chest and stomach, my groin almost decent now with its covering.

'Anyone wants to wash some of the mud of him for me.'

There were no immediate offers and he hauled me to my feet looking into my eyes from less than a foot away. Allowing the belt round my neck to dangle loose he moved both hands to my nipples pulling the clamps off with a jerk then attacking them with digging nails, grinning as I cried and moaned and tried to twist my body away.

'God, I'd love to have you to myself for an afternoon when I come off work. I may be straight but you're enough to cause any hot blooded man to think twice.'

He let go of my nipples and after slapping my face a few times punched me lightly in the stomach then backhanded my face again.

'Get down on your knees and service these fine gentlemen. I need to get soft a bit so I can piss this load in you.' Then grabbing back hold of the belt around my neck, 'I'm not letting you off though.'

He pulled the belt tighter and I started to choke slightly. 'Just to show you what will happen if I think you're slacking and I'll add a boot in your balls to that as well.'

He'd moved his face until was only a couple of inches from mine and then seemed to be staring so directly in my eyes I almost expected him to have X-ray vision and be looking at what was behind me. I don't know what it was but somehow, at that moment, I just knew I could trust him. All right, he was going to hurt me and get off on doing so or watching it happen, but I just knew he was to be trusted to look after me as well, the same sensation I'd always had with John. We stood like that for a couple of moments, just looking deeply into each other's eyes and I saw his shock as some sort of comprehension occurred to him.

He looked away quickly and gave his body a shake, then looked back, 'Just don't ever try and kiss me boy. Then I would kill you.' Then a bit louder as he gave my shoulders a shove, 'Get down on your knees and open your mouth. Don't keep these people waiting.'

I turned round and quickly knelt as instructed being fully aware he was standing close behind me and still holding the belt around my neck. I knew it was my place now to service the rampant cocks flashing in front of my face, also my duty to John but I wanted to get it over with and return to him. If he made me, or should that be if he let me, I'd service his body better than any girl ever had, probably do anything he wanted. He knew involuntarily just which buttons to push. After all, he'd hardly touched me and yet my body and my mind were his to control right then. I couldn't lose him. I had to have him, have him have me.

It was only when an extra thick sweat soaked cock was thrust through my bruised but open lips that it sank in at least two others, possibly more, had preceded it and that I'd obviously been servicing them satisfactorily judging by the cum drying on my face and the fact I'd not been strangled. How could I be off daydreaming about an episode that was unlikely to happen and have no awareness of the present yet act as if all was normal? Well, as normal as my life ever was.

Then I heard it again, that sniveling female voice from somewhere on the periphery of the crowd. 'Karl. When are you going to take me home? You should put your clothes back on and leave that gay perve alone.'

Karl! So that was his name then. Karl, Karl, Karl, it just kept on running through my head as I felt the cock in my mouth start to judder while hands grabbed the back of my head, clutching it forward into another hairy sweaty groin as a stream of someone's hot sweet cum spurted and flowed down my throat, into my stomach to join god knows how many other loads.

'I'll take you home when I'm ready and it won't be soon girl.' His voice, deep for his age, rough in accent and tone, permeated my body and mind. He had no way of knowing it but they were his for the taking. Just my luck to find the right guy at last and he turned out to be hetro.

'You don't think I'm leaving fun like this do you? Bit better than the hand shandy you'd promised eh?'

'You know I don't like it in my mouth,' God how she could whine, 'I want to go home Karl.'

'Piss off then girl. Or I'll drop you off later. Up to you, now shut your gob.'

God! If I wasn't so busy trying not to choke as yet another load of cum was shooting down my throat I might have got off and creamed myself. There was no effort, no raised voice, no false modesty, he was the boss and he knew it. With her and with me. And he preferred me!!! My head was ringing, but that may have been more because he'd taken to slapping it from side to side to attract my attention.

'This lad here says he's got dibs on your ass tonight. That so?' He gestured toward the piss lad from the club I'd almost forgotten about.

'Sorry Sir.' Where the hell did that Sir come from?

He grinned, an almost feral grin with just the hint of humor in his eyes to offset the threat.

'That's OK boy. I'll just have to make do with your mouth then.' My shoulders sagged. 'Don't worry. I've just made arrangements with your master to visit you next weekend and really go to town.'

Oh Yes, another chance. I wanted to shout and cry, I could have hugged him, kissed him. I would have knelt down and licked his mud caked boots, anything he wanted just then would have been only his due.

He must have seen something in my appearance as a sharp tug on the belt round my neck brought me back to my senses. I mustn't shame him, I mustn't shame John either. I would just have to wait. Somehow. He must have been making arrangement with John while I was off in a trance being face fucked.

'Get back down on your knees. There's still a few here need to take a piss and you could do with being washed down.'

Yes there were. I'd only been kneeling a moment when first one, then two, then several streams of piss were streaming over my body, my face and hair, in my mouth when I opened it to breath. I could tell it was required. It seemed my whole body was covered in drying mud and cum, I could feel it sloughing off under the warm streams. Again I was brought back to my senses by a sharp tug on that neck belt.

'Have to get something better to throttle you with next weekend,' he said while leading me over to a picnic table under the trees. 'Lay down on your back, I've just been told what's going to happen next and it won't be nice.' As I lay back he moved behind my head and grabbing hold of my wrists continued, 'God I wish you were mine.'

'I am.' I heard myself reply, or was that just in my head.

I went to repeat myself aloud but found John now holding my head up and bringing poppers to my nose. 'I can see you're off,' he said, But you'll be needing these as well.'

I didn't think I needed anything, just as long as Karl didn't change his mind about next weekend. At least I didn't think so. What had that hetro lad done to me? Why had he arranged to visit next weekend? Or had I imagined it all?

At the other end of the table my legs had been raised and folded back leaving my ass level with the edge and fully open and exposed to the elements. It was no surprise when the next thing I became aware of was what I still considered to be a medium sized cock slid in without hindrance and a hand grabbed my balls. What followed next however, that was different.

Poppers appeared once again under my nose and I had to inhale anyway, thank god I did. Someone laid that bloody leather belt across my stomach with damn sight more than a love tap. My body arched up from the table held only by my outstretched wrists at one end and my balls at the other. I tried to scream but found someone's hand covering my mouth; I couldn't even breathe now, let alone scream. As I fought for breath that belt landed again while my body was still arched up and then I had to allow it to crash back to the table or break my back.

The hand clutching my balls pulled them sharply, 'Get your ass back on my cock you stupid prick,' and he slid back in. 'Can someone gag him; don't want to advertise the bitch too much.'

He thought he was a Master. No way. My original thought back at the club was correct. There was no way I'd ever let him near me again. As if calling me a bitch wasn't bad enough the little prick, and he was a little prick, just had no idea of how to control a boy.

I had no objection to being gagged; sometimes it was necessary, although for Karl I would have tried to manage without, it was just I'd had no warning. Someone's dirty briefs were shoved in my mouth restricting my breathing as I stared back at the piss boy. This time I tried to keep my eyes open when he pulled on my balls and as expected the strap was laid across my stomach again, and then again. He was watching me as his cock plunged in and out of my ass, looking for something he didn't see.

'Hit him harder', as he squeezed my balls and thrust himself faster and faster in my ass. 'Go on, make him feel it.'

I tried to convey the message that I considered him a little shit though it was somewhat of a problem even keeping my eyes open whilst attempting to breathe through the briefs and my clenched teeth. The belt landed several more times over my stomach and once over my tender nipples when I nearly lost it but then a hand reached into view and grabbed it away from him and a voice,

'There's something wrong here. This isn't fun.'

The lad was almost crying as much as myself, 'He's supposed to hurt, to feel pain. That's what he's for. Someone hurt him.'

He was slamming his cock in and out of my hole as if he could hurt me that way. Thankfully someone took hold of his hand and unclasped my balls.

'It's what supposed to happen. You said I could do what I wanted with him.'

'You think yourself a master?' that was Karl's voice of disdain. 'You can't even control yourself let alone a boy like this who's worth six of you any day.'

As my body collapsed back to the table I could feel the warmth of those comments flow through me, helping somewhat to ease the hurt. The hands holding my wrists pulled my unresisting body fully onto the table and then reached over to remove the gag, 'Are you OK?' Karl asked.

'Would have been OK if it was you.'

It was strange looking up to his eyes upside down but the result was the same as before. It would have been different with him.

'Problem is that little twit has killed the mood.'

Turning my head from side to side I could see that reflected in the rapidly vanishing audience sheepishly wandering away. Shortly there were only four of us left, John, someone I'd seen him play with before, Karl and myself.

'But I really wanted you to use me,' I burst out with before thinking.

'So did I boy. How do you feel about me coming back now rather than next week? Get you cleaned up; have a drink, then see how you feel?'

I looked over to John. I knew he would be OK but this was the first time I'd ever allowed back to the house like this.

All he did was look up, mouth the word 'enjoy' and walk off to the truck with his friend. I don't know what checking up he'd done but obviously he had the same good vibes about Karl as myself. As they drove off a pair of shorts and my boots came flying out of the window and he passed me on just like that.

CHAPTER EIGHT

That's how it was I found myself in the early hours of the morning clambering on the back of a motorbike behind Karl dressed only in a pair of denim cut-offs, his T and my old boots plus and assortment of straps and harness.' You sure you be OK back there little boy?'

Good God! Actually I was slightly taller and possibly older than him yet when he talked to me like that how could I be anything else? I just squeezed him back tightly in return and laid my head against his back as off we went. I'd given him rough directions to the house and also a quick explanation regarding John.

I could see there might be problems if this was to go much further and knew we'd have to talk seriously if that were the case but for now all that mattered was he'd get me home and take over. John and I did not have quite the relationship nearly everyone thought. I lost my parents before I ever knew them and through an odd set of circumstances the man some others thought of as my master became my legal guardian before I knew of anything else. Another item I was not aware of for many years concerned the fact the house we lived in was actually mine and there had been enough from their insurance policies to pay for my schooling and upbringing with a little left over.

I suppose I went through all the usual boyhood trials and tribulations, reasonable enough at school to follow on with a minor degree at our local university but I seemed to have a thing with programming computers and by the time this narrative occurs I was, at 23, quite well off in my own right. John had caught me jacking off in my very early teens and apart from telling me to be careful and always to talk to him if I had any hang-ups left it as that. It must have been because he was so matter of fact about that, and many other facets of a single boy growing up without parents, that I later found it easier to tell him of my gay inclinations and later of my S&M ones.

He then came out with the news that he was gay also but was not much inclined to chicken flesh as he called it. Even so, he accepted I would be better off with some training to see if that was really the way I wanted to go, also there some safety in his presence on periodic outings. So it was that at weekends sometimes I'd sleep beside his bed and if he woke up with a piss hard I'd take care of both items. Also we'd built some equipment in the back garden and the cellar where he'd put me through my paces from time to time.

One thing he'd never quite been able to do on his own was make me fly as I called it, though we both knew it should have been possible. We thought it was because, though he was quite happy to use and abuse me if I wanted it, he couldn't really quite get his heart into a private scene and so we came to an arrangement, we both went out separately when in the mood for straightforward satisfaction but when either one of us wanted a bit more something like tonight would occur.

One thing I'd never done was take someone home before. Some of that I'd explained quickly to Karl and now I was flying through the night in a different way, on the back of his bike. I was half crouching behind him to get out of the wind and found my hands creeping up under his leather jacket to discover his lovely hot throbbing hard muscular stomach to play with and warm my hands on.

'You'll going to pay for that later,' he yelled back to me but made no effort to remove my hands so I just held on, occasionally allowing one hand to drift down to his damp crotch. It occurred to me with all the manhandling of my body he'd been up to earlier he must be quite dirty himself under those jeans and jacket and that just made me feel hot. Following my shouted directions we pulled up outside the house and I plugged the code in to open the gates.

Karl drove just inside and then stopped as the gates were closing, I thought he may be having second thoughts either about the situation he'd got into with me or more likely becoming aware of the difference in our circumstances.

'Anyone else at home?' he asked.

'Just us,' I replied. Why was I not worried, he could have bashed me over the head, robbed the house and made off with no fear of being caught. But no. Something had told me I could trust him somehow. Maybe others couldn't, but I could.

'Get off then and give me back my T.'

I got off his bike and pulled his T over my head and handed it to him.

'And your shorts, then turn round' he said with that smile. 'Nothing to get in the way between me and your body then.'

There was nothing in the way either apart from a set of metal rung gates between my body and the well lit main road. The garden was not really dark either as the security lights came on as we passed the gate, luckily not quite fully in the area we'd stopped in.

'Not shy are we?'

He moved toward me unzipping his jacket fully and nudging my naked back with his bare stomach until mine came up against the gates.

'I could tie you up to these gates and fuck your ass raw while people walked past if I wanted couldn't I boy?'

'Yes Sir. Of course you could. Or whip me till I passed out.'

Oh God, here I go again, what I was getting into. More to the fact, what was Karl doing to my brain?

'You really mean that don't you boy?' he asked turning me back to face him, his mouth slightly ajar.

'To you I do Sir.'

I sounded like some stupid silly girl infatuated with the latest pop star. Come to think of it what had happened to his girl? Not my problem.

'Tell you what,' he reached into an inside pocket of his jacket and pulled out what had to be a couple of spiffs, 'Have one of these for now.'

Placing one between my still sore lips he gave me a light and turned my body back round to face the road, pushing it up against the cool metal bars of the gate. I stood onto the bottom cross rung and raised my arms as far as possible before clenching my hands round a higher crossbar, taking several deep drags on the spiff along the way. It was as good as anything I'd ever scored.

'Are you sure you're up for this?' as he slapped lightly at my ass. I grunted and spread my legs further apart while holding tighter with my hands.

'Here we go boy.'

Thwack! Thwack! Thwack!

It wasn't his hand; he'd still got hold of that damn leather belt.

'More boy?'

I sucked so hard on the spiff it was about to burn my lips and spitting it out I answered,

'If you wish Sir.'

'If I wish. Boy you don't know how bad what I wish for could be.'

Whack! Whack! Whack!

He was quite happy to lay that on, and to rub his hand over my hot ass afterwards.

'Nice and red. Oh boy, just what am I going to do with you?'

I wasn't sure if that was really a question aimed at myself so kept my mouth shut.

'I suppose really I should make you count off when I belt you, then make you say thank you.'

'This boy won't say that,' I replied, 'I'm not here to be grateful for your punishment. My pain is for your enjoyment.'

'Do you mean you intend to be a naughty disobedient boy?' he asked. I could hear the grin in his face even if I couldn't see it.

'Yes Sir.' I replied, also grinning.

Just what was it about Karl? I couldn't think of words to describe it, I couldn't put my finger on it. I always enjoyed it when John had a session with me even if he didn't take me where I wanted to go and usually took off when he felt like allowing others to use me, but this was different. He was only doing the same sort of things that stupid youngster from the club had done but somehow he was different.

Oh yes. He seemed to enjoy hurting me and was quite happy for me to resist so he could hurt me more, but he also had a natural realization that things worked both ways and I needed to get something from it as well. I had no idea what it was, just that not only was he more than capable of supplying it, he was also more in tune with me, at least in this respect, after the last hour, than John had managed after all our years and I wanted it from Karl.

'I could get some straps and tie you to these gates,' he whispered in my ear. 'Leave you here all night for any passing car to see. Or maybe I should strap you upon the outside so that can get at your tight little ass boy.'

One tiny little bit of me almost wished he would but I had no time to consider the possible outcome as he'd already managed to wriggle two fingers inside my hole and was feeling around inside me.

'That's tight. As tight as any other hole I've ever tried, thought you'd be too slack for any real fun tonight after what use you'd had earlier.'

'Naturally tight Sir, this boy recovers quickly.'

'That's good. I can see from the state of your mouth it's too bruised for me to use that tonight so I'll just have to make do with this I suppose.'

It was true, now I thought of it. My mouth and my throat did feel raw and bruised; I didn't like to think what they'd actually look like in the daylight, even so I wanted his cock in my mouth. Had I said anything out loud? I may just as well as his next comment was,

' I'll still be sticking it in there for pissing and cleaning boy.'

By now I could feel four fingers, two from each hand pulling in opposite directions, when did he get those up there?

'Is that hurting boy?

I only groaned and he slammed his body forward crushing me against the gate and forcing his fingers fully in.

'I asked if that was hurting boy. Talk to me.'

'Yes Sir. It hurts. Do you want to hurt me more Sir?'

'You really mean that boy?'

'Off course Sir. I'm sorry if it sounds weak but I want you to do whatever you like with my body. It's here for you to enjoy and if you enjoy hurting it then so do I. I just can't help it, I just want whatever you want.'

'That don't sound weak to me boy,' he replied, but you may not like the way my thoughts are going.'

'Try me.'

He said nothing for a few moments, just sticking his fingers as deeply as possible up my hole and I thought maybe I'd pushed him too far, too soon. But then with a jerk he pulled his fingers out and replaced them at once with a hard throbbing cock and putting his arms tightly around me and the gate bars started to fuck me with a vengeance. Several times headlamp beams shone along the road and cars rushed by but that made no difference to him.

'I'm going to fuck your ass for starters, been waiting long enough. Then I'm going to torture you boy, see your body laid out under me writhing with pain, screaming for me to stop. I'll fuck your ass with anything I find, fuck the shit out of you and then carry on. You'll like that boy, you'll let me do anything I want won't you?'

I could only grunt. He was squashing me against the iron gates and every thrust of his hard prick up my ass was slowly squeezing the life from my body. It didn't matter; we both knew the answer was yes. He could do what he wanted; just as long as I knew he enjoyed it.

Karl didn't take long, that first time, and quite shortly I felt the joy of his boiling cum shoot up inside my ass. It seemed to be hotter and stronger than any I'd had before. That had to be false but I swear that's how it felt, as if my backside had been waiting for his deposit all my life. He was sweating profusely and as his body became unstuck from mine I could smell his maleness, my own body was warmed by the heat emanating from his. Stepping down from the gate I turned to face him, to look at him, to see the sweat running down his body, that body I could hardly wait to see enjoying mine again.

Reaching out with both hands I touched his face and ran my fingers slowly down his cheeks, his throat, his chest, then his stomach where I placed my hands flat and used them to wipe some of the sweat from his body and transfer it to my own, slowly spreading this little part of him over my chest.

Then, looking him straight in the eye I reached out and clasping his shoulders pulled my body toward his and laying my head against his neck licked and nibbled at his clean fresh sweat, before rubbing the whole length of our bodies together then slowly sliding down on to my knees and taking his weapon in my mouth to savor and clean. He was still half erect and his circumcised cock filled my mouth and half way down my throat.

'I don't know what it is about you boy,' I head gasping from above, 'you make me want to do things to you I hardly even dreamed about.'

I placed my hands on his ass cheeks; clutching his groin closer to my nose so I could breathe him in deeper and my fingers crept round to that little private hole of his.

'Don't even think of trying that. I told you I'm not gay.'

He made no real effort to pull away though and I used one hand to pull his cheeks apart slightly and the other to stroke my fingers softly across the lips of his entrance, feeling his body buck above me and his cock stir inside my mouth.

'Anywhere your finger goes, so will your tongue,' he warned.

I just pressed lightly on his rosebud to feel his cock jerk and he roughly pulled my head away.

'You're getting me hard already and I've only just fucked you. How do you do it?'

I just knelt back and smiled up at him, which was when he noticed my dripping erect cock.

'Oh! I forgot about that,' he said pointing, 'Do you want a hand job to get off?'

'Why should you bother about me Sir?' I asked. 'It's your enjoyment I'm here for, not mine.'

'You really mean that, you are mine aren't you boy?'

The look of amazement on his face made me want to cry, it looked so innocent and yet there was a force lurking somewhere behind those eyes I knew was just waiting to get out and use me.

'Yes Sir.'

CHAPTER NINE

'You really mean that your body is mine to do what I want with and I can get you to do what I want you to do with no limits?' Karl asked.

'Well, you may have to encourage me sometimes,' I replied smiling, that spiff he given me making me talk far too freely. 'I don't understand it and I'm not going soppy but that seems to be how I feel about you.'

'Can we go inside and get some coffee or something while I think about this?' he asked. I showed him where to leave his bike in the garage next to mine and led him round the back and into the kitchen.

'Coffee or something stronger?'

'Stronger I think, and coffee to keep me awake.'

'When do you have to leave, 'I asked him next.

'You mean I can stay?' I nodded. 'What, use you and fuck you again and again?'

Another nod from me.

'Well, I live above my shop so have to leave here Monday morning by eight. That OK?'

'How about just that drink for now and a quick shower and bed?' I asked, 'Then tomorrow you can have most of the day to you to enjoy yourself.'

So that's what we did, after all I'd been in use for nearly six hours and even my body needed some rest even if I was sure he only had to touch me to make it fly again. Pouring a couple of large brandies I showed Karl down to my den in the cellar. There was a large bed there with a waterproof covering under the sheet and he could see in the shadows some of the equipment John and I had experimented with in the past.

He wandered round looking while drinking, trying to work out what some of the more exotic items were for and, it was obvious, getting worked up.

'Down boy,' I joked, 'Get John to explain in the morning while I cook breakfast if you want. We both need some sleep. Let's share a shower, be quicker that way.'

Karl agreed and removed his boots and socks, dropped his jeans and with no trace of embarrassment stepped into the shower with me. It was a quick shower, as the close contact and shower gel soon had the obvious effects on our bodies. I wanted to be as fresh as possible for him to enjoy when we woke so carefully put a stop to any play, stepping out and handing him a towel.

'You know one problem,' he said. 'This means my body will be all nice and clean when we wake. I think I could get off on me all dirty and you start off nice and clean, then make you clean me up' He paused, and then continued slyly, 'I could always piss over myself in the shower tomorrow morning and make you clean me off.'

I looked up from where I was drying his legs; 'If you throw the pillows and quilt off toward the wall first, there's a waterproof cover on the bed under that sheet.'

The grin that obtained in response was positively evil. Oh roll on tomorrow, well later today. Sliding under the quilt I did wonder if we'd be too hot and Karl obviously did also as he suggested we tried to sleep without covers and I shoved it over the end of the bed.

'Problem is,' he said, 'I've gone and got another massive rod on. Don't know what you've done to me boy.'

I just reached above the bed for the bottle and squeezed a handful of Liquid Silk into my hand, then transferred it without a word to his admittedly hot and erect cock, then turned my back on him facing into the cellar. He took the hint and his weapon probed and slid smoothly inside my hole. Putting his arms round me he started to slowly use my hole to wank himself off. The last think I seem to remember was 'Oh God boy. I just don't know what you've done to me. I've never stuck it up a male ass before tonight'

I know I slept but have no idea how much of what I felt was dreaming and how much fact. I dreamt of fingers and hands roaming all over my body, tweaking my tender nipples slightly, fondling my cock and balls gently, fingers being stuck in my mouth to suck and all the time cocks working themselves in and out of my ass, cock after cock. All the time warm sweet breath on my neck, a tongue licking at my and nibbling my ear lobes and a voice softly 'Oh Christ. Oh fuck. Oh yes.'

Wake up call was a hand shaking my shoulder and John, 'You two look well connected there. Its half past ten so I've brought you some coffee. I'll be upstairs with the papers if you want me for anything.'

'Did you have a good time last night?' I asked.

'Hell yes. You were fantastic and the man I went home with was pretty good as well. Not as good as you boy, but it looks as if I'll have to get used to second best,' pointing over at Karl.

'But he's straight,' I moaned.

John just winked and disappeared.

'What's that I heard about coffee?' Karl's voice came over my shoulder.

I didn't even have to see him, I would have known that voice anywhere now. Just hearing it sent a warm glow through my body it was just that I felt so afraid it could not last.

'Move carefully,' he continued, we're still connected.' So we were, he was still firmly plugged up inside me even if no longer a solid rod.

'Did you get off earlier?' I asked, 'Sorry but I was so tired.'

'That's OK. I went off soon after you anyway but you better never go to sleep on me again boy,' and with his arms still wrapped round me his fingers found my nipples and pinched them with his nails.'

They were still tender and I yelped out loud. He quickly left off and smoothed his fingers over the sore flesh.

'Sorry. Did I hurt you boy?'

'Isn't that what you wanted Sir. I grinned, forgetting he could probably see my face in the mirrored wall, 'But please let this body have time to get up and apply some cream to tender areas.'

'Don't you grin at me,' looking up I saw his face being reflected above mine as he lay across my shoulder, also with that grin of his stretching from side to side of that sun bronzed face. 'You can get your cream later, but first I want that coffee I can smell and then I'm going to get my rocks off. Or rather, you are going to get them off for me'

Karl pulled out of my ass with a plop and turned to lie on his back directing me to sit astride his lower stomach, his half erect cock pressing against my spine. 'That's a morning piss hard you can feel there. Don't see why I should get up if what you said last night still goes. Let's just let things relax a bit and see what happens.'

Those words were all, it needed to remind me I also had an over full bladder and I informed him of that fact even as I continued to drink the coffee. 'That's OK. You piss over me and I'll have to punish you won't I?' There was that sexy evil grin again. 'And of course when you promised to lick up any piss on my body, you didn't state whose piss it would be.'

'I'd love to have someone use a strap on you now or shove a cock in your mouth. I've decided your ass is mine and nobody else gets in there but me but I sure would like to see other cocks fuck your mouth or whop your back for me.'

'I can call John down if you like. He'll strap you for me.'

'No. I don't think so,' Karl replied, 'That would be too odd. He can tell me how to use that stuff over there later and keep an eye on things if you want but I don't fancy the idea of him actually getting off on you anymore. Do you mind?'

Mind! He was talking as if he was going to see me again. I wouldn't have minded anything just then and knew John would be easier at my finally discovering someone to use me, as I required.

'Do you mean this isn't going to end?' I asked grinning back openly and finding my bladder let loose at the same time the stream jetting up to hit me under the chin and as I tried to control it, weakening and splashing over Karl from his chest up and over his face.

He grabbed hold of the heavy chain I'd exchanged with the leather collar last night and pulled my face down toward his.

'Now you've done it boy,' his other hand stretched down to my cock and pinched it across the top, blocking the flow. 'That hurts?' I nodded. 'Good. Boys who piss on their betters are due a lot of punishment aren't they? More than can be applied in one day so I'll have to come back wont I? Now get me clean?'

As I carefully leant forward, clasping my hands behind his head to bring it closer to mine he let go himself with a solid stream of boiling piss I was sure I almost hit the ceiling before spraying back down to shower both of us with his flow. As I first licked his forehead then moved down his cheeks to lap at the piss running down his face he squeezed my cock harder.

'Don't forget. No kissing. I may have a gay boy to play with but that don't make me gay.'

He released my cock and it took off again. We were flooded, the bed was flooded, luckily it had been designed to sag in the middle and I noticed he'd remembered to shove the pillows on the floor.

We both finished pissing at around the same time and he allowed me to sit back slightly then to my utter surprise used his hands to rub our piss all over his body, face and hair, then did the same to me finishing by shoving his fingers in my mouth to suck clean, repeating the movements several times.

'Told you there'd be a dirty body for you to clean in the morning,' he grinned again, 'now get on your back 'cause I'm going to fuck your ass again as you were in such a hurry for me to do last night and I want you to see me do it, and tell me if I do it wrong'

Hell. I had pushed too hard last night, it just never occurred to me at the time he may never have poked a male hole before. Now for it then. We exchanged positions and as I lay back on the soaking sheet I brought my legs back and folded them on my chest. 'That don't look very comfortable,' he said.

'There are other ways but this will do for now if you really want to fuck me again. You don't have to you know.'

'There's no way you get out of it like that. I told you, your ass is mine as of now, I might let someone else beat it,' and he slapped me hard, several times across each cheek to show what he meant, 'but mine is going to be the only cock to fill it. Right boy?' Another couple of slaps, really love slaps compared to what he could do if he set his mind to it, 'Now then. How do we go about it?'

It was strange, directing him to lodge my legs on his shoulders and aim his cock at the rosebud of my hole. 'Now you're ready to rape me,' I said, 'Even so take if slow and careful as you push in, it will probably hurt me at first.'

'Rape you? Is that what I'm going to do? I didn't think this bit was supposed to hurt,' and he made to pull away.

It took a little while to convey the more clinical aspects of process to him and to my surprise he remained quite hard, then I continued,

'Apart from all that there is the fact you are rather well endowed Sir.'

Well he was, especially when seen in more light its present condition. It was one thing to have got my mouth round it with a little space to spare but my mouth opened without a problem somewhat more than my hole would without being forced, how the hell had I managed it last night Then there was I could now see at more like eight inches of the bloody thing.

'I'll leave it then, 'he said.

'Don't be so bloody stupid,' came my reply, 'and you can punish me for swearing at you that later. One, I'm sure you are aware I've been fucked before. Two, you're supposed to be in charge and I thought you wanted to hurt me, within reason,' I finished that one with a grin. 'And three, other people have fucked my ass apart from you; you've been fucking with my mind ever since I first heard your voice last night. You'll have to do a damn sight more than just fuck this gay boys ass if you intend to control him.'

There was no answer, just a quizzical look on his face while he applied a shot of the Liquid Silk I'd passed him and then, looking down, pushed the helmet of his cock at my hole. After all our conversation he was still hard and rampant. Reaching up and grabbing my shins where they lay over his shoulders all that happened for a while was the feeling of that cock pushing at me without any attempt to force an entrance. I don't think he knew at that time how much that was torturing me when I wanted him to get his entrance over and done with.

'Don't keep jabbing like that man, push the bugger through, it won't kill me.'

'It's not that,' he came back, 'I like to see the way your little bud dimples and quivers when I prod it and when I think this here is going to fit in there, like this,' and he did force an entry. Even though my ass had been royally fucked last night and his cock had spent the rest of the night stuck up there I still had to gasp as he broke an entrance. I didn't actually get corn holed as often as you may have thought very often and tightened back up very quickly.

'OK?' he grinned down at me. That bloody evil soul destroying grin.

'Just take it slow please.'

Slow he was but unremitting as inch after inch of his weapon was forced through my ass lips and down into my gut. Somehow he noticed when my grimace of discomfort changed to real pain, or maybe he felt the bone, anyway he just moved his hands down to pull my body up and closer slightly changing the angle to allow, finally, full penetration. His balls knocked against my lower ass and his groin mashed up against my own.

'Holy shit! I never thought the day would come my cock would be stuck right up some boys ass. Never in a month of Sundays'

I knew it was cheeky but the opening was irresistible, 'Its Sunday right now. What are you going to do about it?'

'Later I'll thrash you, but right now, this.'

This was the signal for his first real attack on my hole, and it was an attack, much more so than the previous attempt. There was no finesse now, no wondering how I felt, was I OK?

Not any longer, this was pure unadulterated hunger to get off, with no consideration for the receptacle of that hunger. Right from the start he was pulling almost out and forcing back in, hard and deep as possible. My initial moments of clenched teeth and furrowed brow soon changed to whimpers and moans as he violated me. I'd told him to rape me, and he was. He was animal and I was conquest and he conquered me.

His hands held my hips so tightly I knew there would be bruising but I could look up at his sweating chest, his unseeing eyes, and his clenched teeth and see he had no real idea of the effect he'd had on me, he'd forced his way in and now he was staking his claim, as I'd told him to. His whole body seemed to glow; the hairs on his bronzed skin were all as erect as his cock, every contour of his body seemed in fuller relief than before when he threw his head back and yelled 'Yes! Yes! Yes!' and shot his seed up so deeply inside me, not little spurts but shot after shot after shot, each one I felt collide with the walls of my bowel. He'd done it; whatever happened in the future he'd done it. Last night he'd just fucked me but now He'd claimed me and I was his to just use, however he wanted. Not just now, not for occasional nights here or in the woods, no, it was for every day and every night, for the rest of my life. I just wanted, needed, him to know what he'd done to me, that I'd been claimed.

As we both slowly calmed down and Karl pulled out, lowering my legs back to the bed and sitting between them he wiped a hand across his piss and sweat soaked face and moved to find somewhere to shake off the residue when I caught his hand, pulling it too my lips and lovingly licked it clean.

Then pulling my legs back carefully knelt up myself and lowered my head to his chest, licking his nipples, the runnels down between his pecs and finally bent down to his cock.

CHAPTER TEN

I had only just started to lick Karl's cock with my tongue when his breathing finally calmed and holding my head gently in both hands he raised it back level with his own. Those sparkling clear eyes stared directly into mine, burning right through me and as I stared back in turn I just wanted to drown in them.

'You've been crying,' he said gently, using one hand to wipe the tears from my eyes, 'did I hurt you that much?'

'Yes thank you.'

'But why? Pain if I beat your ass or whip your back or something that I sort of understand, But sex. I thought that was supposed to be different.'

'Oh it can be' I answered. 'Couldn't carry on like this every day anyway or I'd be crippled but I needed you to take me like that'

I paused for a moment considering if I should continue but just looking in those eyes sort of made my decision for me. 'Hang on a moment,'

Jumping off the bed I ran across the basement and pulling open the bottom drawer of my desk grabbed a brown paper bag and rushed back to bed and handed the bag to Karl, then reached behind me and undid the screw clasp holding my neck chain together, removed it and laid it down.

'What's this?' he asked, upending the bag over what was now our bed. This was a heavy fifteen-inch stainless steel chain with small steel rings at each end plus a small brass padlock and key.

'I had this made a couple of years ago when I purchased some of things over in those drawers,' pointing to what I called the interrogation suite. 'The idea is. The idea was.' I didn't know how to continue and dropped my head. I knew sort of what I wanted to say but this was really serious, I'd not known him twenty-four hours and he was straight.

Karl put a hand under my chin and gently raised my head again. 'The idea is, was, what boy?'

Just looking back into those eyes and hearing his voice, I was lost again. He was only a couple of years younger than myself but in his company I felt like a little boy. I gathered my courage and told him just that, also I didn't want him to think me soft.

'After the way I've been treating you since we met I'd hardly call you soft,' was his response, then looking down to my groin 'not that little either.' He made no comment about my other remarks but as I looked at him I thought his eyes were glistening and so I explained.

'I said I wanted you to possess me, fully, own me. You can see this chain is heavier than the one I normally use, it will show over almost anything I wear apart from a suit and the lock only has two keys. One is in the safe upstairs, only ever to be used in real emergency like hospital X rays or such. The other is for the person who places the chain round my neck, the person who I surrender control of my body to. Not quite slave and master twenty- four seven type of thing, though if that is what you want you can have it? '

I'd said too much, pushed too hard. He'd never hinted any situation like this was at all acceptable and anyway, he preferred girls. Why couldn't I have just left things as they were? My heart sank with my head, as I looked away, all I could hear was his heavy breathing and tick tock from the clock on the far wall.

The chain felt cold and heavy as he placed it round my neck and then clicked the padlock shut.

I just couldn't help it; I burst out crying, was unable to stop, and could only kneel there on what was now, our, still soaking bed doubled over and sobbing my heart out. I felt his hand tentatively touch my shoulder then clutch it more firmly when he received no response.

'What is it? What's wrong?' He got off the bed and tried to pull me upright but all I could do was fall over and curl up in a little ball and sob. What was wrong with me? I should be ecstatic. He'd marked me in more ways than one, taken my body, enslaved my soul, and now chained me to him.

Even when I heard him run up stairs calling for John I just couldn't stop though by now it was more just shaking and trembling. I heard them come back down together but I was still frozen in place. I felt ashamed now of my reaction and just couldn't even look at either of them.

'You have been dirty little boys,' I heard John say when he discovered the cellar smelt like a public urinal.

'That was ages ago,' Karl replied, 'and he didn't mind.'

'No he wouldn't,' John continued, their voices coming closer. 'So what set this off?'

Karl told him about the chain and padlock. I heard John take a deep breath.

'I do hope you know what you're getting into young man. There's been several people in the past few years trying to get their version of that chain round his neck and I must admit I never really thought I'd see the day. You know this isn't just a master/slave thing like you read about. If he gave you that and made it your choice, he's handed you control of his mind as well as his body.'

'Yes,' came slowly from Karl, 'I think I realized something of that but what do we do about him right now.'

'Do?' asked John. 'Do? I do nothing. YOU can swat his ass good and strong and then drag him into that shower he insisted in fitting down here and you both get cleaned up and come upstairs for something to eat. Meanwhile I get this mess cleaned up for you, just this once mind you. Somehow I don't think I'll be coming down here much in the future. Go on man, belt his bloody ass will you, it's yours now.'

Basically that's what happened. Karl did belt my backside and then half drag me to the shower where I managed to regain at least some small equilibrium as he washed me down and I had to concentrate in order to return the favor.

Finally, 'You stupid boy. Don't ever frighten me like that again or I really will belt you one and you've already got enough punishments built up to last the rest of this year.'

That nearly set me off again and it was only his use of a towel on my hair that allowed me to disguise the fact. What the hell was wrong, me turning on the waterworks at a moment's notice? I could see, and smell, that John had striped the bed and also disinfected the rubber mattress cover so all that remained was to find something to wear and do as John said, get something to eat. Most of my clothes were upstairs but Karl looked through what little lay in the drawers and picked a pair of very short tight nylon running shorts for me, then finding a pair denim cut-offs for himself with a new sports jock Id pushed to the back as too large for me.

'That will do now, makes you look positively indecent boy. Just about right I'd say. You won't need anything else, its bright sunshine up above. Now let's go get us some food.'

That's basically how the afternoon continued. It was just gone midday when we surfaced and John had a salad lunch prepared and waiting with a bottle of wine so we spent the next few hours sitting in the garden and getting things sorted out. John gave Karl a book to read I'd never know he had, well to look at pictures mostly, showing how he could make use of the stuff downstairs and the frame setup in the garden at weekends. He pointed out that a heavy session could cause temporary damage to my body so Karl had to monitor himself as well as me and leave at least a week for me to recover.

We showed him round the house, it was on three floors, four if you count the cellar that was only really a half cellar, just that I'd blocked up the high windows in my play half and other room was used for freezer, wash machine and storage. Ground floor was a through kitchen and dining area leading out to garden one side and my office on the other. First floor my proper bedroom; again with a big bed that Karl smiled at, large en-suite and over the hall my main living room. Top floor I explained was John's self-contained flat and I told them both I wouldn't be going up there anymore.

It turned out Karl actually owned his motorbike shop, with a mortgage true, but the business was his and he employed half a dozen staff and lived above the shop to save money. Most of whom he told me were also gay as he seemed to get on with them better, one in particular early twenties and half colored who'd given Karl a blow job quite a few times but was really more into being the active partner and into kinky sex though, and here came that sexy grin again, never from what he'd told Karl as extreme as last night. 'Might invite him over one weekend later on, 'Karl said, 'He can have the top and I'll have the bottom. Right boy?'

'Whatever you say Sir.'

John offered to move out but we both told him no. I was too used to having him upstairs and sharing meals and evenings at times. That may change a bit and I knew he had his own friends anyway but as I pointed out, he'd always liked to watch and I actually knew his mate did as well. It would be up to Karl from now on if we had an audience or not.

We spent the rest of Sunday just getting used to each other, making arrangements and consuming two more bottles of wine till finally Karl said 'Work in the morning,' and took me off upstairs to bed. A bed I'd never shared with anyone before but after he fucked me and we curled down, my back to his chest and his strong arms round holding me safe it seemed somehow the most natural thing in the world. Oh yes, he fucked me first, 'I'll fuck you any chance I get,' he told me, 'but not like downstairs, that's for weekends. But I usually have a wank at least a couple of times a day and your tight little bum feels much better and you did say it was mine.'

I slept like a log again, dreaming of sensitive nipples, hot breathing and hard cocks then woke to the alarm and Karl turning me onto my stomach for what he called a 'morning quickie.'

He put his dirty jeans and T on for breakfast asking if he could bring a change of clothes back that night and telling me just to wear the tight running shorts I had yesterday. 'Have something nice to look at over breakfast,' he told me, you can change into something more suitable after I leave.

That's how the week progressed. He came round each night after work for dinner. When he mentioned having to go home to catch up on paperwork I suggested he bring that round and we started transferring his accounts to a computer system. He wasn't computer illiterate, just had never had the time to sort something out. I got fucked almost every night and every morning, a mini service he called it, and we were both looking forward to Saturday night and the weekend to see where a major service would take us.

CHAPTER ELEVEN

Saturday finally came round. I couldn't have been more apprehensive, having tried all week to discover what Karl was planning, what I should wear, what I should prepare for, how I should react.

'Don't you worry about it boy,' was all he would say as he tugged on the chain round my neck, 'Just remember you're mine now, the weekends mine and what I decide to do with you is mine to decide as well. You just make sure to have a meal ready for me as normal.'

As he left for work that Saturday morning he passed me a carrier bag. 'Open this at midday, change, no cover-up allowed, be ready for me at the normal time.'

Then he waved and roared away on his bike. It sounded as if the clothing choice problem had been solved for me though I did find it difficult to put mind to anything else apart from that bag over the next few hours.

Spent the morning catching up on work, it only took a couple of hours a day if I kept on top of things. John came down and told me his new friend was coming for lunch and spending the weekend and that Karl had invited them to join me for something to eat about one o'clock after which they would stay and leave us to our own devices. Midday chimes finally sounded and I rushed back in from the garden to open Karl's bag. Oh God! He had been busy, reading the book John had passed over to him, and rifling through my drawers downstairs.

Padded wrist and ankle restraints OK!

Upper body harness and then the ring to go behind my cock and balls with a strap round my waist with tie rings attached and another strap to fasten behind my ass. OK! I had hoped he would experiment with strapping me down sometime.

Heavy solid half-inch metal ring to fit round my scrotum above my balls continually weighing them down. There was a note attached, these stay on all weekend. Was I getting excited or nervous? Not really sure. Just keep going!

Then I pulled out my clothes. Clothes? I'd cobbled this together last year for fun, a one inch wide leather belt to fit my waist to which I'd attached a couple of chamois leathers roughly one foot by one foot. This wasn't clothing. My thighs would be quite naked apart from the two belts and any movement I made at all would cause the chamois to swing about showing more than it hid.

The phone rang. I switched to speaker. It was Karl. 'Put them on boy. You hear me?'

'Yes Sir.'

'Good. It's still very warm. I suggest you invite John and his guest out to the patio for lunch,' Shit. I'd forgotten about them and in my dismay missed his next instruction.

'I'm sorry Sir. I missed your last instruction.'

'O boy!' Karl came back with. 'You better start listening. Any infractions at the weekend will be punished. Get it. What I said was after lunch get them to help you fit the sling up outside and then you can get my dinner ready. I'll be eating outside tonight.' He just put the phone down. It rang again. 'Better eat yourself before I get home, I'm going to have fun and you won't have time yourself.' Line went dead before I had time to reply.

What did he mean by no time to eat later? Why did I have to dress like this when he wasn't here to look after me? What had he planned for the weekend? He'd been fucking me regularly all week, one end or the other, but as we'd decided, that was just sex, weekends were for enjoyment. What did he classify as fun? What did he think of me? Was I only his kinky gay boy? I just didn't know any more, it seemed I didn't know anything.

All that sort of thing was flying through my mind as I made my way up from the cellar, dressed as instructed and started setting up outside for the lunch I'd prepared. We'd decided, well Karl had, that weekends we would live in the cellar and ground floor. After all he'd said, 'That's where the games room is, all the equipment I may need, Widescreen DVD's, bed if I allow you to sleep and kitchen so you can feed me, so no need for anywhere else.'

There was a cough from the open door and John asked 'Are you ready for us? Can I call Pete down?'

That was the first time he'd ever asked to enter my part of the house. It had never mattered before, after all he'd seen me naked, used and abused countless times and I asked him 'Since when do you ask to come in?'

'Since now,' he replied. 'Karl did tell me to check on your dress though.'

I could feel myself blushing. How come I felt I embarrassed in front of him now after all we'd been through before?

'Well, I have to obey him now don't I? For God's sake call him down. I'm starving.'

To tell the truth I just wanted to get the initial meeting over and done with and stood as still as possible beside my chair. Everything was ready on the table and I'd not have to move once sat down, well not for a while anyway.

A moment later Pete followed John out onto the patio. It was the first time I'd really seen him although I knew John had a friend who occasionally visited the club, but he'd never been to the house before. The similarities with myself were obvious. Tall, thin, dirty blond hair, but then we started to differ. He was older than me by about ten years, body more wimpish; obviously didn't exercise that much, wore glasses and the most obvious today, wore knee length shorts and a polo top.

I directed him to the table while attempting to partially hide myself behind my chair but he looked at John who nodded at him and then walked round to hand me a sealed envelope. On it in Karl's handwriting, which I already recognized, was the message; Open, Read, Obey! Inside there were several folded notes with different messages on the top. One said, open before lunch and continued inside, John's friend may examine you fully, go to him. Only his fingers may enter your ass if he wishes in which case you will clean them for him afterwards. He may use your mouth in any way he sees fit. Now pass him this note to read.

I looked at him, looked at John; it was obvious they knew what the note said. My face I knew was bright red, I'd never been so embarrassed, and this wasn't a scene in the club or down the woods or even in the basement. This was a cold command instructing me to submit myself to a stranger, Karl was nowhere around for me to see. This just wasn't right; he was treating me like a piece of worthless trash he could use or discard at will. This wasn't about sex, this wasn't about enjoyment, and this wasn't even about me. This was about Karl's ownership and control of my body - and it would seem, my mind.

I looked once more at Karl's handwriting and passed Pete the note.

'Thank you,' he said and tucked it in his pocket, then walked forward and tugged me away from the chair. Lifting the chamois half shielding my cock he looked at the restraints and fondled my balls then after sticking his fingers in my mouth and telling me to soak them told me to bend over. Flipping up my rear covering he stuck one then two fingers up my ass and wriggled them about. I didn't dare look at John; my whole body I could feel was red with embarrassment. He removed them, told me to stand up, and then stuck his fingers in my mouth, telling me to clean them, then, walking back to the house 'I better go and wash my hands before eating.'

He was so cold and matter of fact about it all, and Karl wasn't here, I didn't know if I should be insulted or how to react. I looked over to John who'd already seated himself and was pouring the wine. All he did was ask if I wanted a glass and then as I carefully sat down with my skimpy coverings really giving me no protection and knocking the weight round my balls he just said, 'It's up to Karl now isn't it? Actually I told him you'd never go for it, you have surprised me'

Pete returned and just sat down as if my dress and his slight examination was par for the course. It did take a little while for the conversation to start flowing and I'm not sure any of us were really at ease that first time but by the time we'd finished the second bottle and I got up to make coffee I did feel a little less embarrassed about my dress and being so on view and they appeared more at ease also. That was to change for me quite soon. John cleared the table while I brought the spare sling up from my cellar and we quickly fitted it to the frame just off the patio as Karl had instructed me earlier, of course they both knew what use it would probably get later and I was flushing red again even before I read the next note.

It read, after coffee go and kneel on the grass beside the patio. Pete & John should both need to visit the toilet now and can piss all over you. You may not wash afterwards. Hand them this note.

Oh Karl, you were asking one hell of a lot from me on such a short acquaintance, you supposedly straight and just getting ideas from a book. My body was now burning up with embarrassment. Was this how our lives were to continue, you telling others to use me like trash, is that my reward to opening my heart and soul to you, handing you unreservedly control of my body. Just because I've fallen in love with you but didn't dare tell you?

Even so, I found myself kneeling where he'd stated with my head bowed.

I got pissed on. I didn't look up to by whom but it happened more than once. After all, the operative word was - unreservedly. It's what I'd promised him.

CHAPTER TWELVE

I knelt there for a short while, drip-drying as it were, and considering my situation, the situation I'd placed myself in. Had I been looking too hard and misread the state of affairs? Was I placing too heavy a load on his shoulders? After all, up to last weekend he'd considered himself straight with just the odd blowjob from another man. What did he consider himself now? Straight with a functional mouth or ass to fuck every night until he met another girl? Was this weekend going to occur just because he'd have a boy to slave for him and who he could beat up without any risk and then boast to his mates about? Had my emotions overridden my senses?

All I really knew was the erection standing proud from my drying body made a mockery of the little chamois cloth supposed to be covering my privates. Come to think of it I'd been either erect or half way there most of the time John and Pete had been around as well. Karl was fucking with my mind it seemed and I just didn't know how to react. It came down to trust and I realized that after a whole week I still didn't know him at all. So how could I allow myself to trust him?

He'd spent several evenings talking to John on the other side of the room while I was getting his books into shape. I'd overheard John telling him what a contrary kid I'd been and how it was when he'd noticed that I seemed to be going out of my way to be naughty and would always change to my running shorts when John intended to spank me that he'd become aware of my interests. Ha! Interests he called them. I could still be contrary, that I knew, it was in my makeup. I also knew without any shadow of doubt that I felt very sexy. It wasn't just my erection that wanted sex; my whole body was starting to vibrate deep inside somewhere looking for a release I wanted but knew could improve with waiting..

It was when John taped my shoulder and handed me another note I realized I'd been kneeling there for ages attempting to sort things out in my mind. They still weren't properly sorted, that would have to wait, and the sight of Karl's untidy scrawl on the outside just sent a warm glow back through me. Raising my head I looked up at John with a stupid grin plastered over my face, I didn't care what I looked like.

'I think you've got where you want to be at last lad,' he said. John had called me nothing but boy for quite a few years but when my face responded to the change he put a finger to my lips, 'That's over now and about time to. You can be a proper boy to Karl, you two need each other, we were only playing at it and you know that wasn't really enough. We're leaving now and I'll spend the night at Pete's, you two have fun.'

'You don't have to move out,' I told him. After all, he'd brought me up from a baby and was all the family I had.

Was he mind reading? 'You've new family now lad. I'm invited back for lunch tomorrow so let's chat then. Tonight's for you two. Have fun.'

My chest filled up with emotion as he walked away. I knew he was right and he was overdue to live his own life but he was still family. We'd have to talk it over with Karl.

That thought itself was a bolt from the blue. One of the biggest decisions I'd have to make, emotional, practical, all the rest, and my first thought was I'd have to talk it over with Karl. Not just for his advice but for his agreement. Oh Karl, you have fucked with my life haven't you? I just hope I'm worth it.

Then I opened his note. Oh Hell! I couldn't see to read past the first line at first, I just burst out crying again. Not sobbing, not gasping to breathe type, just crying, I felt my eyes fill and spill over as my chest burst and I finally struggled to my feet, knees almost locked solid from kneeling in the wet grass there for so long.

'Hope you've spare storage space boy, I'm moving in.'

I had to sit back down where I was, luckily still on the grass, as I couldn't see. I'd crumpled his note in my hand and had brought it to my nose trying to smell his scent; I almost crushed it in my mouth, remembering just in time there were quite a few more lines of instructions written there as well. I managed to get a semblance of control back, wiping my eyes with the back of my hand and carefully straightened out his note, luckily still just decipherable. I couldn't carry on like this; he'd soon get fed up if I burst into tears at any moment. Pain tears maybe but I was sure he didn't want the other type again. I just couldn't help how he affected me.

'Hope you've spare storage space boy, I'm moving in.

You can help me unload the van later.

I'll be home around six, have my dinner ready.

I'll eat on the patio and you'll sit by my feet, ready to serve, where you belong at weekends.

I intend to enjoy my weekend boy.

You won't.'

PS

'Wash your hands. I don't want stale piss on my food.'

Why did the promise of pain and degradation make me cry with joy? After that first line everything else was a bonus.

Finally I made my way to the kitchen, and then had to stop thinking too much about what might lay ahead as time was short. I set the table for one on the patio with a couple of candles and two bottles of opened wine set in a bucket of ice. His dinner was chicken salad so I prepared a plate and being almost six laid it out ready with a cover. I had a small foam backed bath mat I put down beside his chair just in time as I heard my truck, now our truck, pull up out front so I sat, cross legged, beside the chair with my head bowed. Now at least I knew why he taken the truck this morning.

It seemed ages before I heard footsteps and then a set of bare legs shod only flip flops appeared before me. I could smell him, his sweat from a day's hard work, natural man sweat. I wasn't usually into the ranker side of body odors or other outpourings unless well into a scene but I wanted to lick him clean. To wash his body with my tongue. I'd start at his feet and work slowly up until I could look into his eyes. I just wanted to look at him but he placed a hand on my head.

'Keep your head down boy.'

He sat and from the corner of my eye I could see one of his muscular thighs, topped off by the bottom half of a well filled pair of thick cotton shorts. A couple of inches of material led up to the bulge I wanted to service. The scent I picked up on now was more than sweat; you get that sweeter man smell round the crutch from a man, a mixture of sweat, piss drips, pheromones, something. I could almost feel the heat rising from his body, the heat that would keep me warm tonight whether we touched or not. But I wanted to touch him.

'You smell rank boy. Did they piss on you then?'

'Yes Sir.'

'Did you do everything fully I instructed boy?'

'I think so Sir, I tried but you will have to check with John, or Pete.'

'Good boy,' he continued, reaching down to place a brand new metal dog bowl before me and then poured an inch or so of wine in to christen it. 'You deserve a drink then,' and he placed his hand back on my head forcing it down to the bowl.

126

I would rather have been drinking from his body but bent right down and lapped from the bowl as I guessed he wanted.

'You can use your hands to pick the bowl up boy. Everything you eat or drink this weekend will be in that bowl unless I feed you by hand, and everything that I put in that bowl you will consume. Yes?' He slapped me round the back of my head.

'Yes Sir.'

'You stink too much. Crawl over to the sling and show me how you get into it. Don't look at me!'

How could I not look at him? I was dying to look at him; I just wanted to look in his face, to drown in his eyes. Oh! Wanted him so much it hurt.

Somehow I crawled over to the sling hanging from the frame where John and I had fixed it earlier and standing, with my head still bowed, managed to lay back and adjust my body to the position where my asshole would be fully exposed when/if my legs were raised and tied off.

All I saw of him was a quick glimpse of his body as he stood, naked above those tight shorts, a slight line of dark hair showing on his bronzed body and leading from the rim of his shorts to his belly button and mirrored by an even finer sprinkling between his pecs. I never got to see his face. 'Close your eyes,' he called.

I never heard him on the grass but knew the moment he stood beside my head and turned to face the scent.

'Head straight and eyes closed,' this with a harder slap across my face.

Then a small blindfold so all I had was my sense of smell to go on, that somehow had become even more acute. Straps fastening across my chest and arms pulled up and outwards to be likewise fastened off quite rapidly followed that. My head he left raised and loose, laughing as he slapped it from side to side, 'Better leave some part of you able to move.'

Then he transferred his attentions to my legs, likewise lifting, bending and tying off, finishing with a strap across my groin, just above my cock.

'Have to see about stretching this a bit I think,' as he bashed it from side to side. It was still half hard. Wouldn't the bloody thing ever go down? 'You just hang on there for a moment. I've something to set up I made at work. I think I'm going to enjoy this.'

Enjoy What? I started having second thoughts again. I felt my pulse rate and breathing speed up. What was I doing putting my body completely at the mercy of this strange hetro, bi, man I hardly knew. He could do anything he wanted. But that was it. He was supposed to do anything he wanted, anything he would enjoy. I'd handed him my body for his own personal enjoyment that was the arrangement. I thought of his last note, I thought of him and my breathing eased.

I never heard Karl return, just became aware he was standing beside my head again.

'Better now,' he laid his hand on my brow. How long had he been there, watching me, reading me?

'Relax boy. Now we'll get things interesting.'

[[For those of you waiting impatiently for the heavy sex and punishment to return - it's on its way. Boy had to wait so thinks you should as well]]

CHAPTER THIRTEEN

I heard Karl grunt and whisper to himself as he moved about doing something to the top of the frame the sling I was tied in hung from. All I had to go on were his little noises and occasional brushes of his body against mine in a non-threatening way.

Then, 'That should do it. Thought I had the measurements right. 'Better have a drink boy,' his hand behind my head and a wine bottle held to my lips, 'Go on. Drink deep; I've still got the other bottle.'

He must have encouraged me to swallow a couple of glasses before my chokes took precedence and he let my head back down.

'OK. Let the entertainment begin.' Even through my blindfold I could see he was grinning.

I heard a match strike and the smell of sulfur, the heat of his body touching mine across my chest when he reached somewhere above, then another match struck and the same contact closer to my groin.

'This should be fun. I need to relax for a bit.' I heard wine being poured into a glass from somewhere about head level on my right, then his breath on my face from the same side.

'Any moment now.'

Ouch!

He was holding a candle above my chest, allowing the melted wax to drip in my body.

Ouch! Ouch!

Moving it around, my chest, my stomach, my groin.

Oh! Ouch! Again and again!

He must have one in each hand. Another match struck. 'Be lower soon.' How could he be speaking in my ear and yet have hot wax falling on my body from several positions. Were we alone?

Karl did it again, read my mind.

'Just you and me boy. His fingers were caressing my brow, across the blindfold, my cheeks, and my lips. 'I think I want to see your eyes,' the blindfold was removed.

His face was just a few inches from my own, his eyes looking at mine as they blinked in the low sunlight, his brilliant teeth showing in a grin. His breath of wine and smoked chicken salad wafted up my nose. I wanted him.

He turned his head to look toward my raised legs and I saw he'd contrived a metal bar to clip across the frame to which a large number of candles had been attached, flat to my body, some of which were lit and dripping down on me. Ooohh! On my cock, then another and another. He'd lit a set that was dripping all over my cock and balls. The very little movement my body had to move just allowed the drips to cover me more thoroughly. It was almost worse with my eyes open as I could see which candles were about to drip down next.

'Look at me,'

I looked back up, all I could see now were his eyes, his face was so close, he breathing out straight into my mouth, I was inhaling his air, his fingers roving all over my face and then holding my hair,

'Are you hurting boy?'

My eyes must have answered his question, and then his hand gripped my hair so tightly I yelped, and his mouth covered mine.

Oh God! He didn't kiss boys, or men for that matter. He wasn't playing about either, his tongue dug straight in and attempted to wrap around mine. He was trying to get his head inside my mouth and if my hands had been free I'd have done everything possible to help. I'm sure there had been no intention of kissing me, and was well aware that his reactions when he did so were as much a surprise to him as the very idea of him kissing was to me. I was aware at exactly the moment his brain caught up with what he'd been doing and there was a slight pause and he went to pull away, then changed his mind and dug in again. Finally he had to surface or run out of air but remained bending over me with a look of amazement on his face.

'That's a turn-up for the book! Where did that come from?'

'Do it again but keep your eyes open please,' I gasped quickly. I knew I shouldn't be giving him instructions but just couldn't let him get away.

His lips met mine again, this time more gently and as I carefully stuck my tongue in through his lips and brushed it round his teeth I fought to keep my eyes open and looking back into his. Have you ever kissed with your eyes open? It's not the natural way but the reward can be so fulfilling. Whatever I felt for him before, whatever submission or promises I'd made, they were nothing compared to now. What I saw in those eyes, the eyes of the man I'd handed my body to, the man who intended to hurt me, who was in fact doing so right now; my body still jerking to the hot wax dripping onto my groin, that mans eyes were full of such joy and incredulity. I just couldn't let him escape and attempted to suck hard on his mouth and tongue when, suddenly, as he took a breath, his tongue forced mine back and dived deeply back into my own mouth now trying to reach those parts of my throat usually only reached by a cock.

I've no idea how long we kissed, one of his hands holding my head up slightly, the other roaming over my upper body, picking at the wax, drying now the candles had stopped burning. Finally he pulled away and stood up to massage his stiff neck, looking down at me the whole time.

'Phew! Just what is going on?' he asked.

I didn't dare hazard an answer, didn't care where it came from, just hoped it wouldn't spoil things for us.

'Whatever,' he continued, 'There's something here needs attention and that can fill your mouth better.'

I didn't know when he'd removed his shorts but had felt his aroused cock knocking against me earlier and as he moved behind me and released the section holding my head up I was able to admire it more closely from an upside down position.

Having my head hang down backwards was not the most comfortable position, neither was it most conducive to breathing, but it sure as hell gave his cock deep and easy access. I realized afterwards he was so sexually hyped up his actions were almost automatic. My head fell back when he released the straps; his cock slid straight in and down causing me almost problem in swallowing and his fingers seemed to find my nipples without looking. Nipping and pinching them deeply cracking through the cooling wax his flexing thighs clenched round my head and he just stood there breathing heavily.

His cock was throbbing in my mouth, a throbbing I could feel emanating from his whole body, and his fingers were clenching and unclenching round my nipples.

'No! No!' he was gasping, 'This isn't right. I shouldn't be doing this.'

There was nothing I could say, all I could do was clench my lips tighter and try to swallow him. That did it, sent him over and he started shooting, still with my head jammed upside-down between his thighs and hardly moving apart from his hands that were now thumping at my chest.

'Bastard! Bastard! This is wrong; I'm not a sadist. Why am I doing this?' He was still shooting down my throat, but I could feel his body shaking and he was crying as well.

Karl's paroxysms slowly ground to a halt and he pulled out of my mouth without a word, then quickly went round the sling released the holding straps and sat down on the grass. I managed to slide to the ground, my legs didn't really want to respond so quickly but I had to get to him and half crawled, half stumbled toward him.

He was still crying a little and used one hand to wave me away, the other to wipe his eyes. I paid no attention; this was not the moment to hold to our agreement about the weekends.

'Don't,' I knelt before him and reached out to hold him but he batted my arm away.

'Sir. What's wrong? Please let me help.'

He flew at me without warning; one punch caught me on my cheek, the other as I ducked the side of my head.

I don't consider myself weak and in other circumstances would have fought back but even in these circumstances knew I must never hit him that would have finished any possibility of salvaging our relationship. I attempted to clasp his arms but that left his head free to try and nut mine so I had to allow one arm to protect me there leaving one of his free to continue pummelling my body. We were rolling about on the grass, on and off the patio, the table went over, and finally back on the grass crashing against one of the massive posts holding the frame.

I was trapped underneath and saw him raise a clenched fist ready to bring it down when he looked down and froze.

'What have you done to me?' he cried out, 'you've turned me gay, I don't care anymore about that, I want to live with you and was about to move in. You let me hurt you and I want to do more. That's not right, I'm not that sort of person, and I don't go around hurting people. Especially someone I love.'

Someone he loved?

There was a flash like summer lighting, but felt through my body rather than seen through my eyes and everything froze for a moment. I ceased attempts to protect myself and let my arms fall away, He could have bashed the hell out of me right there then and I'd have let him.

What else could I do?

I risked it. Reaching up with both hands I clasped them behind his neck and pulled his head toward mine, at first he was resisting, I saw the first tiny bit of understanding in his face as he realized I was stronger than he realized, that in a real fight we'd probably be equal. As that knowledge percolated through to his brain his body lost a little tension and when he was close enough for me to lick at the tears still showing on his cheek he slid his legs back and lay fully over me.

'You could have fought back harder,' he said, a touch of question in his voice.

'Ssshh!' I kissed his lips softly.

'Why didn't you fight me? I nearly bashed your face in.'

'You didn't, that's what matters,' was my reply, accompanied with another kiss.

'But why don't you fight back? You could, I can tell that now. Why do you want me to beat you up? Why call me Sir? It's not my scene'

'Let's take it backwards,' I said, 'It is your scene, look how hard your cock is and you've only just finished fucking my mouth.'

He brought his lips down to mine that time.

'I don't want you to beat me up as you put it. I want you to hurt me. That's different, I can't explain it but I need to be abused not just by someone but for someone, for someone I trust fully to care for me. John was that someone before but now I've met you I know what was missing before, I want you to hurt me. I take the pain for you, that's where I fight back. Accepting it for you, and it works for you as well, I know it works for you, I knew it last Saturday night,

134

there's a connection between us when you hurt me. Something I've never felt so fully with anyone else. I can't really put it into words but that's how it is.'

I'd never tried to put my feelings into words before, had never even considered how to describe them, after all I'd never met anyone like Karl and wondered if they made any sense to him. I knew they did to me and couldn't bear the thought that a misunderstanding might break what was, for both of us, a new relationship.

Karl lay over me just thinking for a moment. 'I do get off on hurting you, I have to admit it. But I don't want to tie up any lads at work and beat them. I know most of them are gay, I've even had a few blow jobs off one.'

'I should hope not,' I looked up at him, 'The connection is between us and it better be my body you use next time you feel randy. I will fight you tooth and nail to keep that position; I've no intention of sharing you with anyone.'

Of course,' I continued with a grin, 'If you want to share me, at weekends that is, then it's your call. I told you I was yours and that's why at weekends I'll call you Sir. Karl lives here during the week and fucks me when he feels like it. Sir lives here at weekends and can do what he wants with boy. Can you understand what I mean'

He kissed me again and lifting up looked back at me quizzically, 'you know Karl has fallen for you boy?'

'Boy is grateful Sir. He has been speaking with far too much freedom and feels very unutilized right now.'

OK! That was a bit cheeky I know, and I did reach down and grasp Karl's cock rather hard so I suppose I deserved the couple of heavy slaps and 'Shut your mouth then,' he gave me.

CHAPTER FOURTEEN

After a little while Karl got up, reached down to yank my chain, and we set the patio back to rights. When he put his shorts back on and went to get some fresh ice for the last bottle of wine I rushed down to the cellar and quickly grabbed some items to shove in a box I thought he might find useful and got back just in time to drop them by the frame and sit cross-legged before his chair.

When he'd sat down with a fresh glass I scooted forward and stuck my face in his warm crotch whereupon he hung his legs over my shoulders trapping me just where I wanted to be. I could raise my head and look up at his stomach and chest or stare directly forward breathing in his warm musky scent and sucking on the outline of his cock.

He taped the top of my head, 'Don't suck and get my shorts wet. Just sit there. I've some thinking to do.' He seemed to think for ages and I wished I'd put the mat under me, the flagstones had become very hard, when his legs moved and he pulled on my hair to make me look up, 'Are you sure this is what you want boy?'

How do you answer that? It's not what I want that matters and it's not my position to answer a question like that anyway. My opinion counted for nothing right now.

All I could think of to do was get up, walk over to the frame; turn away from him with my head bowed and reach up to grab hold of the rings above my head. I stood there for a while willing him to react, not looking up, trying to guess what he was up to when I finally heard some movement.

I flinched when his fingernails dragged down my back to the cheeks of my ass.

'Maybe,' I heard him mutter, 'But how do I? Oh Yes.'

He must have noticed the clips attached to the rings and reaching up attached my wrist restraints in place so if my hands lost their grip my spread-eagled arms would still be held in place. Then dragging at my legs he pulled them apart and clipped them off the same way.

I was still looking down when his crouched body appeared below me and his hands were pulling and twisting my balls, examining the straps containing and separating them and causing me to gasp. Looking up at me,

'More?'

I nodded, and he attached both the weights Id earlier flung quickly in the box. That would teach me to look more carefully another time. Karl set them swinging slightly and stood up, now dragging his finger nails over my chest and stomach, then kneeling and repeating the performance down my inner legs. It's amazing how much more sensitive the body seems when held in such a vulnerable position and my body was almost rippling in reaction to his nails when he stood and dug them into my sore nipples.

I tried to bite back on the cry that called forth but with limited success, Karl twisted harder, then with no warning, let go and started slapping my stomach from side to side, slowly working his hands up my body, over my chest and finally to my face, He wasn't holding back very much and I was being thrown about by the force of his attack, my teeth were clenched tightly and my breathing very ragged by the time he stopped for a breather.

He wrenched my head back roughly, 'Look at me boy,' and he held a strap in front of my face before laying it over my shoulder, then removing his grip on my hair let my head fall free while he picked something up and wrenched my head up again.

'I said to look at me,' and this time he held out the cat before laying it over my other shoulder. 'Any last requests?'

Oh that grin. There really was a touch of the feral somewhere behind it.

I could feel the endorphins had started to work somewhere deeply inside me and Karl's equivalent were obviously working on him, the light flush and tightening of his skin, I felt a joy that I'd not been mistaken in feeling we had a link, a link hopefully about to be strengthened, he intended to hurt me; cause me pain, and I had to take it, stand up to it, to show him, make him proud. Proud of me for tolerating whatever abuses his imagination could think of, and, as importantly, an acceptance of himself, of how his exploitation of my submission to him would bring us closer.

That's how I fought back, not physically but by accepting the pain, living with it, allowing it to consume my body as Karl would consume, would breathe in the pheromones and neurotransmitters I knew my body would shortly be emitting, helping to make us one.

'I said any last requests?' that punch to my stomach would have doubled me up if not spread-eagled as I was. I'd taken too long.

'Gag me please,'

I didn't want our neighbors calling in the police suspecting murder. I might have a large secluded garden but sound traveled at night. He allowed my request and picked up a ball gag, holding it before my eyes as he spat several times over its head before jamming it in my mouth and fastening the strap tightly behind my head. I'd smelt him when he raised his arms and now I could taste him, almost refused the poppers he held toward my nose so as not to lose that scent.

Luckily I didn't. After holding it to me for several inhalations he sniffed at the bottle deeply himself and after re-capping it struck without warning, left and then right, with the belt across my chest. A quick look into my eyes and he nodded, 'Good,' he half whispered to himself and moved behind me.

CHAPTER FIFTEEN

Nothing happened for a moment, for a longer moment. I tried to listen; nothing, to turn my head where I could; nothing, was he there? What was he doing?

'Eeehh!' His finger nails scratched hard down my back, over the cheeks of my buttocks and down the backs of my legs, then turned and lightly scored their way back up to my shoulders, a breath in my ear.

'You hanging around for me boy?'

My body had reacted far in excess of the discomfort he'd just inflicted but the next reaction was more in keeping.

Crack!

Crack!

Crack!

Three quick belts across my ass cheeks with the strap, the first causing my body to flex forward and the next two following so quickly it had no time to swing back, just bent further in half in a vain attempt to escape. The gag had been necessary; I would have yelled the place down.

Bottle of poppers appeared back under my nose and this time I breathed in with relief, if he intended to lay it on like that, right from the start, I'd need all the assistance I could get.

'Warming up nicely now,' hot breath again in my ear accompanied by nibbling on the earlobe and a hand passing over my sore cheeks.

Of course he wouldn't be able to see very well, it was getting dark and the solar lights cutting in would show little detail on my back and the under lighting on the patio would actually put us into shadow.

There was no time to consider possible lighting problems as the next set of blows landed across my shoulders and back followed by another pause. I waited for the heavy breathing in my ear, waited, and waited,

Hell!

Whack! Whack! Whack!

Another set across my ass cheeks. This was double torture, not knowing where or when the next blows would arrive.

'Didn't expect that did you?' Karl's breath rate had increased; there was an touch of something different in his voice, it was more guttural. He dangled strips from the cat over my face, 'Do you want to play with this next?'

I couldn't see him but heard the real question in his voice and nodded.

'This will really hurt you, do you want poppers?'

I shook my head, no. Shock, surprise, on my part at any rate. I didn't want any artificial assistance; I wanted to feel his abuse of my body to its fullest extent. I had to, for me and for him. I had to show him.

It seemed my senses entered overdrive, I actually heard him step back, heard his breathing stop for a moment as his arm pulled back, then the swish as he brought it down and the cat lay hard across my shoulders, again, my back, and again, my backside. He moved close and ran his hand from shoulder to ass.

'Better,' was that to me or to himself?

I was quite well aware when he stepped back again, this time directly behind my body rather than to one side, my ears seemed as enhanced as my nose and I knew exactly where he was standing. I knew just what he intended, if not gagged I may have started pleading, I hope not but who knows. I somehow felt it when he adjusted his stance, took a deep breath, held it for longer than before, and then, letting it out with a gasp, laid into my defenseless body.

Starting at the top he swung that cat back and forth across my shoulders to include my arms, lower back, the tips curling round my waist, lower still across my cheeks, then back up again. I lost count of the strokes half way down, was not even aware I let go my grip on the rings above my head and only hung from the wrist straps.

Even so I was still aware of his breathing becoming almost as strangled and spit flooded as my own poor attempts through the ball gag, at least twice he hawked and spat the contents of his mouth on my back; I swear I could hear his heart beating.

It was only when I felt his hands lift my head gently and undo the straps behind my head I became aware the animal noises intruding on us were actually a continual stream of sound emitting through my mouth as it attempted to gasp enough oxygen in to live while still protesting the abuse. He pried my eyes open with one hand.

'Look at me.'

All I could do was look. Even if I'd had any breath spare to speak I had no words. Just sounds, moans, muffled screams, cursing, all muddled up and escaping in that dreadful continuous spluttering sound.

'You OK?' he asked.

I nodded.

'Shall I let you down?' Head shake.

'More??'

He grinned with that question, his eyes staring directly into mine. He grinned with his whole face, somehow his whole body was happy.

When that grin was aimed at me I'd have done, allowed, anything. I knew at that second I'd have to warn him about it. If I ever saw him look at anyone else like that I'd kill them, and probably him as well. That was one part of him I could never share with anyone else that look was mine. I nodded with, I knew, a stupid inane grin on my face. I couldn't help it, I didn't care. The tears now running down were a mixture of pain and pride and joy, I neither knew, nor cared, which.

He reached up and placed my hands back on the rings then turned to go back to the house. He must have heard the change of tone in my muffled gasps, I didn't want him to leave me, I needed him close, I knew it to be stupid but if he was close he eased my pain.

'Hang on there, only be a moment.'

How was he so attuned to my thoughts and need?

He returned shortly with a toped up ice bucket and the last bottle of wine, no glass. Removing my gag he picked out an ice cube, placed it in his mouth and then, gently kissed my lips, transferring the cube though to me with his tongue. Oh it was nectar to my mouth, so cool and refreshing; I crunched, swallowed and looked pleadingly at him for another. He laid his head to one side with a quizzical look, and then picked another to place within my lips, then with yet another reached down to my balls which were still heavily strapped and weighted. To tell the truth, before he touched them I'd quite forgotten they existed.

'Take them off?'

'Please sir,' I answered.

They'd been there so long I no longer had much feeling but as he had to twist the straps to undo the straps that changed. They were bruised, tender, and sensitive as hell and I had to respond. Each twist, each undone clip drew a little yelp from me that I just could not hold back. What would happen when the blood flow resumed?

Karl happened.

The second he released the last stud allowing the straps and weights to fall to the ground he rose like a rocket and with one hand behind my head jammed his mouth over mine, the other hand still holding the ice cube grasping my balls viciously.

His body was tight against my own, damping down my paroxysms, the night air was comfortable but cooling from the days heat yet he was burning, the heat from his skin almost burnt. I could feel his heart beating fast, in time with my own, almost sense the blood being rushed through his system, was sure I could hear it. Or was that mine?

His open mouth absorbed and swallowed the muffled screams issuing from deep inside me as blood resumed its natural flow through my cruelly over abused balls. We exchanged more than just tongues or spit then. Who knows what it was? Pain, strength, endorphins, pheromones, whatever? We exchanged something, something more than body fluids, something that we became aware of at the same moment. His body locked momentarily and he pulled his head away slightly.

'Did you?'

'Yes,' I grinned back. I had to do something about my stupid grin.

'Have you ever...?'

In the heat of the moment I interrupted him, 'No.'

'What...?'

'I've no idea. Can you live with it?'

'Oh God yes!' He continued, 'You know I've got to fuck you soon?'

'Fuck or rape?'

'Oh rape!' There was both threat and promise in his smirking reply. I'd take both. 'Where?' he continued. I glanced over my shoulder to the sling. 'What about your back?'

What could I say? My back and ass cheeks were still burning and against the sling would be sore as hell but I wanted, needed him inside me. Deep, thrusting, painfully inside me. He'd fucked me before but this was going to be different, that had really been consensual. I needed him to take me so forcibly; aware he was hurting me, he must consummate his possession of my body in the most primeval way possible, as my body would absorb and consume the result of that consummation.

'I've an idea,' he said.

CHAPTER SIXTEEN

Yes, he did have an idea. First bending down for the bottle of wine he took a swallow, then drank and held a mouthful, bending forward and squirting it into my mouth, continuing in this fashion for several mouthfuls finally replacing the bottle and holding his face close, his hands behind my back.

'Here we go.'

Once again his mouth closed over mine just as my breath exhaled under protest with a yell because he'd placed his hands full of ice cubes against my bruised and beaten back and was dragging them back and forth, freezing and exasperating the welts at one and the same time.

He pulled away slightly, bending to allow his hands to wander down to my ass cheeks.

'You bastard!' I gasped out and he moved the handfuls of ice to my balls and caressed my groin and between my legs.

My body was trying unsuccessfully to dance away and I kept on swearing at him, calling him all the names I could think of.

Up he stood and held one palm flat across my swearing mouth, half filling it with the remaining ice, now mixed with my own scent and sweat. Karl closed my mouth and while I crunched and swallowed the taste of my own essence he repeated the abuse on my body twice more. Then he bent to release the shackles holding my legs apart, and as I shuffled my legs back together reached above me to release the wrist shackles. I just couldn't help, it, as his sweat soaked armpit brushed across my face my tongue flicked out to lick at the small array of fine black hairs nestling right in the deepest part, licked and swallowed, licked and swallowed, stuck my nose as closely as possible to breathe him in as deeply as I could manage.

He finished and put his arms round me, 'I thought you weren't keen on tasting stale sweat,' he commented.

'I'm not,' I'd surprised myself. He wasn't stale, he was Karl, that was different and I told him so.

'You silly boy,' he responded, 'you can let go those rings now.'

'I can't.' My hands were still clenched tightly around the rings over my head and I seemed unable to open my knuckles sufficiently to let go. Finally Karl had to reach up again and force my hands to open whereupon I half collapsed against him, my arms now falling over his shoulders, my head resting against his.

'Are you sure you're up to this?' he asked, a little worried.

'You've got to now. You don't get away so easy after what you just did to me.'

'I don't get off easy?' he exclaimed, while helping me half stumble over to the sling and, with some care, lay back, my head in its own cradle, while he raised my legs into their slings. 'Will you need strapping down?'

'No,' as I lifted my arms to grab chains above my head. 'You'll need more light,' and I nodded at the candles above me he'd not lit earlier.

'Haven't you had enough?' he asked.

147

'You need to see me, you must see what you are doing.' I meant that on two levels but could tell that initially he only understood the visual one.

Walking slowly round the sling he was tipping the remaining ice cubes over my body where most of them slid down to jam along my sides, then he repeated the walk, this time lighting a selection of candles that covered the area from my upper chest down to my groin just above my once more erect cock. Leaning over my head as the first candles started slowly dripping he kissed me lightly, almost a feather against my lips, and returned to his position between my legs.

He was softly lit from two directions, the under lights from the patio behind him and the flickering candles above me, throwing his glistening body into a strange relief. I would have sworn I could see some type of glowing nimbus surrounding him, I could certainly feel and smell the heat he was giving off as, giggling slightly now, he was forcing ice cubes through my hole. The violation was uncomfortable and the wax now dripping more regularly over my body was painful, even so I found myself smiling to see him so enjoying himself.

He spat twice in his hand and wiping that over his cock for lube followed the ice by thrusting the head of his cock straight through the lips of my hole, no foreplay with it this time. I gasped but he never looked up, just watched what he was doing and slowly kept up the pressure and thrust until his groin and mine met. Then he raised his head looked back at me, my face, my eyes, and clicked.

It sounded to me an audible connection; a band snapped into existence between us, I felt it thrum from his body to penetrate mine down to the bone where it echoed back into his, back and forth through the joining together of his cock ploughed deeply inside me.

He felt it then, I think he finally fully understood the realities of our relationship. Even though the inside of my ass was slick and ready his cock hurt and he could see the steady drip, drip of wax at different places over my chest and stomach was causing me to grit my teeth against crying out. But I'd managed to keep my eyes open and through the candle light caught hold of his, my view narrowed down from his sweating body to his face where I could see droplets of sweat run down from his brow, drip of his chin, but my view narrowed down further, to his eyes, where I tried to see into his soul and allowed him full access into mine.

He shook as the impact hit him, I couldn't let him look away. This might be my only chance; I had to get through to him to his subconscious, to his unconscious, so he'd know this was how it should be, how my inner self thrived on, craved for, the abuse and pain he inflicted, and, as importantly, how much his self was my opposite half as John, or any other fly by night sessions, had never been.

'I get it!' was all he said.

It was all that was needed. He knew it all now, on every level. It must have hit him hard but he didn't stop.

His cock started slowly and most thoroughly fucking my ass. I could feel every inch of it ploughing me open, deep oh so deep inside me. Pull back, almost out, and then heavy slow thrust back again, brushing through any obstacle without regard. This ass was his to use as he liked and he intended to prove it, his eyes now running with tears again, still locked on mine; pulled back slightly now to include his face, that slightly feral grin had returned and each time either his cock or the dripping wax hit a new spot causing me to gasp through my clenched teeth his grin grew larger even through the tears.

'Oh Yes, I get it all now. I hope you never regret meeting me.'

I would never do that but as he was talking his slow and comprehensive fucking increased speed and changed to that rape he'd promised earlier. He reached up himself and grabbed hold the set of chains above my legs that matched the ones I was gripping tightly above my arms. Some of the candles had finished or gone out but that mattered little. His cock grew and throbbed inside me as he reamed me, down to my core.

All the time his eyes locked onto mine, it was me now who couldn't glance away. He was bashing my balls with every inward thrust, my teeth were no longer clenched, I would have ground them away, instead I heard myself, 'Oh fuck, yes, go on you bastard, harder, make me yours, I am yours, use me.' I was also moaning, my body was twisting and turning at his ill treatment but I wouldn't have had it any other way.

The sweat was flying from his body, and the spittle form his mouth, both covering my body. I found myself crying again, not so much from pain as from some strange form of joy and so was Karl.

'Yes boy. You are really mine; I'm fucking you so deep I'll shoot out your mouth. I'm going to fuck you anywhere I want; your mouth and ass are mine. Yes! Yes! Yes!'

God he shot. A great massive stream of hot strings of little Karl's so many and so deeply inside me I was sure some would never escape. Still he was fucking and shooting, covering my whole gut with his seed, marking me as fully inside as he had my outer body earlier.

Finally he slowed, his cock shrinking slightly, and stood, still holding the chains, gasping for breath and looking down on me.

'I think that makes you mine boy. Nobody else gets your ass again, in fact nobody gets anything without my permission now or the whipping you just had will be a pleasant dream. Right boy?'

'Whatever you say Sir.'

'I didn't ask you to agree,' I felt him flex against my outstretched legs, 'You have no choice,' he continued, 'Your answer is Yes Sir. Or keep your mouth shut unless I say otherwise. Right boy?'

I nodded and felt him flex again, then my bowels were filling rapidly with another boiling stream, one this time that seemed never ending. The increased pressure against my own bladder had its own result and my erection just fell over as my own cock released its own load of piss straight up in the air and catching him under his chin.

'I never gave you permission to let that out,' he said grabbing my flapping member and aiming the stream at my face and open mouth.

He leaned forward, directing the slowing stream all over my body and as it dribbled to a stop using his hands to make sure I was covered everywhere. As he bent over further to stick his piss soaked fingers in my mouth his cock escaped from my hole with a plop.

'You better move Sir,' I could tell I'd be unable to retain the flood for long.

'Never said you could speak boy,' his fingers pinched my over worked nipples and as I threw my head back and gasped my bowels let loose. A stream of Karl's piss and cum and who knows what of mine, flooded out, I heard the flood crash against his body and splash back against my ass cheeks.

'You are a filthy boy,' his hands moved back to my cock, now my bladder had emptied itself once more painfully erect. 'What do you think I should do about this then?'

He grabbed my balls in one hand and stretched them, with the other squeezed my cock tight. I kept my mouth closed, well almost and only answered him with a little yelp.

'That's better boy. Now let's have a closer look.'

He knelt down; I could just see the crown of his head peering between my raised, outstretched legs and feel his breath against my cock. One hand was still pulling and twisting my balls but the other suddenly stuck several fingers inside my hole, and then......

I did scream. Only a little scream but I couldn't help it. Karl's mouth engulfed me. Not fully, not swallowed right down, but he slid his hot lips over the sensitive head and took several inches into his mouth and started to suck. I had no chance to warn him. I came, came in his mouth, a massive load; it had been building all evening. Even though he pulled away and continued to bring me off with his hand Id still cum in his mouth.

This lad who a week ago would have settled for just a hand job from the local bit of skirt had stuck his fingers up my ass after I'd emptied my bowels over him. Had sucked the first cock in his life, and now I'd had the nerve to shoot in his mouth.

He stood up and reached forward, one hand wiped the remains of my load across my face while the other released my raised legs, then two hands grasped mine and pulled me from the sling to stand upright against his sticky, slimy body. He bent his head just that little bit to place his closed lips against mine, then, as I opened my mouth to meet his, fed me back the cum he'd retained in his mouth.

He pulled me with him and lay down on the ground, my body part sliding and part sticking to his. There was little light but I could see his open mouth and grinning teeth just waiting for me to kiss and nibble.

'You're a filthy boy,' he told me when we had to pause for breath.

'What about you then,' my fingers found a sting of cum lying across one cheek and I scraped it toward his mouth where he sucked on my finger.

'Had to do it sometime didn't I, just seemed like a good idea,' he told me.

I think we could have both stayed there for ages, our filthy bodies drying slowly, just holding each other and kissing lightly but Karl recovered hi senses before me.

'We'll have to move. All this to clear up, and ourselves. I better see to your back as well. Don't forget we got guests for lunch.'

With a groan I rolled off and slowly managed to get to my feet. He was right, it turned out in our future that he often was, but just then all I wanted to do was have him cuddle me. Luckily there was little cleaning to do, a box of toys to be cleaned in the shower with us, he cleared the table and set the patio back to rights while I used the hose to wash away all signs of our party. The sling we left out to drip dry and finally turned the outside lights off and made it to the shower.

I couldn't help but laugh for a moment, we were both filthy, our bodies covered in grass cuttings, mud, god knows what, but I stopped laughing when he got me holding on to his broad shoulders while he washed me down. It was a continual series of whimpers from me as he gently washed my hair and then sponged shower gel over my body before carefully turning my body under the water flow to rinse off. I seemed bruised and hurt everywhere.

Even drying off was impossible and in the end he used the hair dryer as much on my body as for my hair. Finally he had me stand while he sprayed glorious ibuprofen all over me. While he finished cleaning himself and the toys I went and poured a large brandy, then just managed to make it to our mattress and collapse.

He joined me shortly and held the glass to my lips, sharing the alcohol as we'd finally shared everything else this night. I lay my head in the crook of his arm and licked his brandified lips.

'Would you mind if I sleep facing you tonight Sir. I don't think my back could take being touched much.'

He just pulled me closer and was kissing my face when I fell asleep.

I had the most wonderful dreams of being held and knowing I was loved. A voice told me I was loved, that I was safe now. That I would always be safe. A tongue was licking my face. In my dream I knew it was a dream, as my dog had died the previous year. Even so, I snuggled closer to my dream; it felt so good like that.

CHAPTER SEVENTEEN

The morning came too soon. In fact it was John's voice calling from the door that finally broke through my befuddled senses.

'Lunch still on at two sons?'

He called across the room. It was strange him no longer calling me boy after so many years but I knew I was more boy to the man still sleeping beside me than I had ever been to him.

'What's the time?'

'Almost twelve.'

'That should be OK then,' I replied.

A couple of hours would normally be enough time but as I tried to stretch the memory of last night returned, as did notice my body was somewhat damaged and not as supple as I'd wish. Managing somehow to force my eyes open I discovered myself still lying on Karl's arm, looking him straight in the face. He must have dropped off almost immediately as I had.

Sleeping he was a different man than the one who'd so thoroughly used me last night. I'd not noticed before just how thick his eyelashes were, they showed more with his eyes closed. His dark untidy hair fell all over the place; the natural curls showing more in an un-brushed condition. His lips, slightly open to show those teeth that even in repose appeared to be smiling. He was breathing slowly and deeply, and I moved my head just sufficiently to breath in the air he exhaled and watch my lover sleeping. He was my lover, my first one, hopefully my only. Those others had just been sex partners. Would our connection still be there or would he have second thoughts?

'Have you seen enough?'

I glanced up to see his eyes wide open and returning my look. How long had he been awake?

'No Sir, never. But we need to get up and I think I'll need your help, my backs locked solid after your enjoyment.' I risked it and kissed those lips I'd been watching so closely.

'I suppose a fuck's out of the question then?' Thank god he was smiling.

'That's for you to say Sir but we have guests for lunch and not much time.'

'Yes. I heard him.' So he had been awake after all.

Karl managed finally to rise himself with much creaking of joints and after helping me lay face down sprayed my back again with ibuprofen after which I carefully and slowly got myself up, washed and emptied. Breakfast was just juice and coffee but by the time I'd sunk a second cup I'd decided my body would probably recover, given time.

Karl, it seemed, had a different idea as to what my body required. I'd stayed naked so far but when I went to pull a pair of shorts on he stopped me.

'Wear what you wore yesterday and put these on underneath.'

He handed me a short leather strap to fit behind my cock and balls plus a small leather jock two sizes too small. What I wore yesterday was roughly two pieces of chamois, each just over a foot

155

square, hanging from a thin belt round my waist plus wrist and ankle straps. They made me feel almost more naked than when actually so. I looked back at him. The weekend Karl was back. He slapped me lightly across my face.

'Do it boy. Your holidays over for now.'

Luckily it was another glorious day outside and I set the table up under the trees for three and placed my rubber backed mat beside Karl's chair. When he brought the salads down he saw my seating arrangements and came over to me where I was removing the sling and clearing the odd items missed from last night.

'I see you know where to sit boy.'

I went to answer him but he put his hand behind my neck and kissed me, his tongue playing catch with mine and his other hand moving down to gently massage my butt. When Karl kissed I sure as hell knew I'd been kissed, if I'd had to choose a way to die that would have been it. I wanted to forget lunch and have his cock take the place of his fingers, a slight flexing and two digits that had been exploring my rosebud slid straight in.

Releasing the vacuum hold on his mouth for a quick breath I moaned.

'Yes.'

That must have brought him to his senses as the fingers were withdrawn and my backside slapped once hard enough to feel then my open mouth filled by those same fingers.

'Clean them boy. Shut up, suck them clean and listen well.'

I had little choice, one hand still behind my head and the other stuck in my mouth, I was unlikely to be going far.

'Unless I give you permission you will not speak except for Yes Sir until I say otherwise. Don't worry, I intend to have your ass later, I'd give it a quick bang now but there isn't time. Now go and get the wine and bring your bowl back with you. You can also bring a cushion if your bum is still sore from last night.'

'Thank you Sir,' gained me a grinning Karl and a backhanded slap across my face.

'I told you only Yes Sir. I'll allow that phrase as well though but no more exceptions. Now get busy.'

Turning round to go and collect other items for lunch I saw John and Pete on their way down. They must have seen what just happened, the house was behind my back so Karl would have seen them; probably that was his intention, to set our positions straight before others.

Twisting back I saw the little grin I'd half expected and dared to dart forward and give him a quick kiss before running back to the house. He followed more slowly and met me half way back with my arms full of wine bucket, my bowls and a cushion. I was half expecting a slap or thump somewhere but all he did was grin and mutter under his breath.

'You really are a silly boy.'

One more trip and everything was ready, I stood beside Karl's chair waiting for his permission to kneel down. It was already feeling more natural to be on display as and when he wished, to be waiting for his orders. I was still embarrassed at my dress and situation being publicized as it were but that was what he wanted and I had to obey. Also, under that too small leather jock my cock was attempting in vain to escape, causing a pain that contained elements of ecstasy within it.

He motioned me down and I knelt, the cushion between my legs to soften the pressure on my backside. The conversation above my head seemed unreal, there was no mention of me apart from an early enquiry about the state my back, and otherwise it was as if I was invisible. After a while Karl handed me down a bowl of mixed salad and sliced meats, I was not surprised when there was no cutlery to accompany it.

I knelt there beside him holding the bowl in one hand and eating with the other. Every so often his hand would reach out and ruffle my hair, and each time he did so warmth seemed to flow from it encompass my whole body, all I wanted to do was trap my head between his thighs and breathe him in, to have him hold me tightly.

I wasn't aware at first when my bowl was empty, that they had also finished and his hand was resting permanently on my head. I did realize my body was almost quivering with a joy that needed venting somehow, I think at that moment I would have obeyed any instruction he'd given me, no matter how demeaning. As it was, 'Get another bottle of wine boy,' had me jumping to my feet and with a quick 'Yes Sir,' running back to the house and then returning with a fresh bottle and opener. I wasn't even prepared to stay away from him long enough to open the bottle.

He told me I could kneel and resuming my previous position I removed the cork and handed the bottle up to be told to hold out my bowl which was then half filled with wine. He must have read my mind.

'You can start with the real stuff boy, and I'll supply the recirculated version later.' I felt like crying.

I wanted to cry because I'd just been told he intended to piss down my throat later on. How sick was that? I didn't care; it would come from him, which was all that mattered.

Lunch over he told me to stay and finish my bowl and the others helped him clear everything away. Karl returned alone, another almost full bottle of wine in one hand and a metal case in the other and told me to move myself and seating over to the play area.

Then he sat cross-legged before me on another cushion, just looking and taking the occasional swig.

'You know,' he said, in a quite normal tone of voice, 'Fucking with your mind like that was fun but fucking with your body is more satisfactory. That's next.

CHAPTER EIGHTEEN

He stood up and took the case behind me and after some fumbling placed a hand on my back, 'Raise your ass up boy,' obviously not high enough as his hand moved to jerk on my neck chain, 'higher.'

I felt the tip of a dildo or butt plug positioned at my hole and his hand moved to my shoulder to push down slightly.

'Now get your ass back down on that.'

He reached forward without any further speech and grabbed my right hand, pulling it back to clip the leather wristband to my left leg, then my left wrist to my right leg. Now it was only my knees that held my ass away from what I now realized was a dildo and I also knew with the angle my body was now bent backwards they would be unable to hold me up for long.

That I should slowly plug myself was Karl's intention, he told me so on his return to my front where he sat watching my face.

'I don't see why I should do all the work when you're quite capable of hurting yourself for me to watch.'

After the invasion he undertaken of my ass less than ten hours ago you'd think I'd find taking a dildo up there an easy option. That was not the case. He'd lubed it well; even so I was finding it painful and difficult to allow the intrusion while though my thighs were already complaining about the strain. He decided to help things along, firstly by attaching a pair of nipple clamps, then holding a bottle of poppers under my nose, and finally putting his face right up to mine, his hands on my shoulders and telling me.

'Get your ass fully plugged or I'll hit you boy.'

That all helped and I managed to sink my body back down till my ass cheeks were resting on my ankles. That hurt enough and I didn't want to sit any deeper down until my body had time to acclimatize. Karl bent forward and looked behind me the sat back and grinned, that little half grin that I'd come to realize was a sign of his other side, what I thought of as his animal side.

'That's cheating,' he said, 'Get your ass right down on that cushion I allowed you in my mercy.' I shook my head.

'You know I'm going to hit you then?' I nodded.

'You want me to hit you?' I shook my head.

'But you'll let me?' I nodded, and smiled.

That smile may have been a mistake as one hand darted out to grab my hair strongly and the other was used to swipe across my face, back and forth, back and forth, time after time after time and not holding back much on the force either. Then he let my head slump and switched to my stomach, some light punches followed by slapping till it turned red and heated up.

'Must remember to get gloves before I hit your face again,' he murmured, 'less chance of damaging my hand then.'

Damaging his hand? What about damage to me, I couldn't help whimpering and moaning, the tears rolling down my face, my head hurt, my stomach hurt, my ass? My ass had swallowed the dildo right the way down and was now sitting cheeks flush to the cushion. At least one thing was better.

Karl noticed when that happened and stopped hitting me. He gave me another sniff of poppers and as the buzz hit put his tongue out and licked the tears of pain from my face. He said something about, 'We should share everything, good or bad,' and then he kissed my brow, each eye, and briefly, my lips.

Oh Karl! Do you really know how you affect me when you do something like that?

It didn't matter; he had another idea. A connection from my neck chain back down between my ankles pulled my head backwards restricting body movement even further and making it almost impossible to see my groin without causing probable strangulation. His fingernails scratched down my chest, dug into my nipples, then continued over my sore stomach and bypassed my achingly erect cock to score down my thighs.

Was it my slight moan of disappointment, the look on my face, or just common sense? He looked down at and slapped at my cock with his hand.

'Did I miss something out then boy?'

I kept my mouth shut; or rather kept my thoughts to myself while my lungs labored to draw in sufficient oxygen.

'You didn't expect me to service your cock boy did you?'

He'd slid back and bent down, looking at my cock from a matter of inches whilst continuing to bat it back and forth.

'You must be stupid boy. I abuse you and yet you stay hard.'

He was really hitting it now and at times including my balls. My moans were becoming more distinct and turning into little yelps. I couldn't help it.

'Bout time I filled your mouth with something to shut you up.'

He sprung upright and placing first one leg then the other over my shoulders forced my body and head to strain further back and somehow tightening the chain round my neck in the process. I was already having some trouble in breathing when his rampant cock stuck itself in my open mouth and part way down my throat.

'You shouldn't have any trouble swallowing at this angle,' and he slowly thrust his cock into my mouth as thoroughly as the dildo shoved up my ass.

It was a matter of accepting the intrusion and allowing it full access or strangling on my neck chain as my head was forced back more and more. I accepted it, it was easier to swallow his cock right down, gagging in the process but did he have to strangle me and break my back in his enjoyment.

Karl stood still as a statue and holding my head tightly rocked it back and forth, using my mouth to wank his cock. This was different to my giving him a blowjob, it was even different somehow to having my face fucked, he just stood there, saying nothing and using me, as he would once have done his hand. His groin smelt of fresh Karl and sweat, my eyes focused on the dark wiry hairs as they pulled back and then crushed my nose again, and again. I had to concentrate on something else than my bent back and I anyway loved the smell of fresh Karl at any time.

His thighs clenched either side of my head and I felt his cock in my mouth throb and shot, one, two, three times straight down my throat where I couldn't taste him. Then he managed to pull back and continued, swamping my mouth with his juice.

'Don't swallow boy,' and stepping away he knelt down watching me swirl his juice round my mouth. 'Now open your mouth and let me see it full of my cum.'

As I obeyed from either side of my full mouth a mixture of his juice and my spit escaped and ran down to drip from my face to my chest.

'You are a dirty boy,' he said as he cleaned his cock down with his hand and then wiped that through my hair.

'Your dirt Sir,' I smiled up at him after swallowing the last contents of my mouth.

'Better give you some more then, close your eyes and keep your mouth open boy.'

Oh Yes! It didn't get much better, drinking, then to be covered head to foot with his piss, would make me really feel like part of Karl when he covered my body with what had so recently been part of himself. Sure enough, a few moments later a hot stream of acrid piss hit the side of my face, quickly being steered into my open mouth. As that filled and I swallowed he walked the stream around, in my ear, through my hair, down my back, the other ear, then back to my mouth to finish off. Oh heaven, I was soaked with Karl, stank of Karl and, after he used a towel to wipe my brow and eyes, looked straight at Karl.

'You enjoyed that boy?' I nodded with, I just knew, that smirk on my face. 'Can't have that can we?'

He rummaged around in that case again and came out with a short cardboard tube he stuck in my mouth and told me to grip with my teeth. Then he came up with a candle he proceeded to stick in the tube. Oh! I could see where this was going, yes, there followed the flick of a lighter with the flame being applied to the wick which soon flared away.

'You can move your head up and down but if side to side you'll meet this, he showed me his fist. 'And if you spit it out I'll use that belt on your front like I did your ass last night. You hear me boy?'

I nodded, the first drips of wax falling from the end onto my upper chest.

Karl saw that and moved behind me to slacken off the chain. At least I found it easier to breathe now. On the downside the wax would now fall almost directly onto my cock and balls, my tender cock and balls I discovered.

He sat down cross-legged before me with the wine bottle in one hand.

'This is going to be interesting.'

163

CHAPTER NINETEEN

Karl just sat there looking me straight in the face, taking occasional swigs from the bottle and periodically sharing with me as he called it by swilling a mouthful round his mouth and spitting it out over my body.

I, on the other hand, attempted look directly into his eyes, to take strength for his obvious enjoyment, a task that became more and more difficult as hot wax started to drip onto my cock and balls from the lighted candle stuck in my mouth. I had a little movement available back and forth but he didn't want to see wax dripping on the ground between us, he wanted to see it drip on my body, wanted to see my pain. I knew it was showing, the wax was hot and still melted as each drip landed on my cock and balls, which in their turn were still sore from last night. Each slight sway of my body back and forth caused the dildo up my backside to respond in turn, pressing and rubbing a slightly different part of my bowel each time.

Then I saw it, that sudden flash across his face as he became ever so slightly more aware, aware it was more than just seeing me in pain he was enjoying, aware we were connecting again on that level neither of us had known existed before.

I'd known something of the sort was possible from the first time he looked straight into my face as I stood before him in that mud pool last Saturday but he'd had to find his own way here, I knew he wasn't a natural sadist, not even if only for the weekend, though his imagination had surprised me. It was almost that he'd been working on automatic and was only now looking to see where he'd been. Hurriedly he moved to take the candle from my mouth, then behind me to release my restraints and helped raise my body to eject the dildo before returning to sit before me, his legs opened and bent behind me, holding me between them.

He looked at me for quite a while, almost begging me to talk first. Finally, 'What is it? What happened there again?'

'I don't really know,' was my reply. 'No. Wait,' I continued as he began to object. 'I really don't know but I'll try and explain if I can.'

'You better,' was Karl's response. 'Something happened just then.'

'It's started happening since you first really hurt me, back in the woods. I felt something then, I knew you were different right away.'

'You mean because I'm hetro,' he asked with a smile.

'No,' I replied. 'It's something to do with endorphins and things, and you and me, we connected last night somehow and now all you have to do is set me off and we seem to connect again. Anyway, you're not hetro or you wouldn't be here now thinking about sticking this little bit of yourself up my backside.' I gripped his cock lightly which had risen back to attention as if he'd not emptied his load over my face a short time ago.

As Karl lay back I thankfully rose to straighten the kinks in my legs and then lay back beside him, my head on his stomach blowing hot breath over his cock that I was gently mauling about with my hand.

I explained to Karl that many years back I'd discovered I got excited if John had to punish me even though I had no idea why it was happening and being something of a wild boy he'd had to punish me quite often. Then I'd started doing things just so he'd put me over his knees and spank me and he soon caught on to my behavior. Being gay himself and at that time twice my age he'd stopped using that form of punishment until, a couple of years later, I'd been about sixteen, he'd caught me one day trying to hurt myself in order to get off. We had some very open talks over the next week with the result a few years later that Karl had come across. John was still a bit uncomfortable about hurting me much himself or having sex with me but quite enjoyed watching others abuse me. I was happy because I felt safe with him there.

Karl's cock was responding more strongly to my ministrations and I left it alone, turning my head to lick at his stomach, then turning right over to lay between his legs and stretching my arms up to play with his nipples. I could feel his hard cock twitch and flex against me, could feel his strength there, and in his firm hands as they grabbed my head and half dragged my body up so my tongue could replace my fingers on his nipples.

'And? What has that to do with you and me?' he asked.

I told him how most of the time it was just a scene and sex but that occasionally, I didn't know how or why, something would happen, and after a while I would feel this sort of separation of mind and body, almost be looking at myself being whipped or abused as if from a distance. It still hurt, in fact usually hurt like hell, but I was able to damp the sharpness down to a dull throbbing and always wanted more. It seemed to be only when the other person got off on abusing me, me as a person, not just me as an available body with a pain loving streak.

Then found myself unable to continue. How could I explain something I only half understood myself? Also the realization had finally just exploded in my little brain that this was more than a sexual relationship, strong though that was. I really was in love with Karl, not just his stiff hot cock throbbing against my groin, not just his firm body lying under mine, not just his hands that could hurt me or his lips that he'd kissed me with, not even those deep eyes I could get lost in. No! It was Karl I'd fallen in love with, Karl the person, Karl the whole. My heart had known it last weekend, after that first night. It was only now my brain had caught up. I wanted to yell it aloud for the entire world to hear, I wanted to tell him, to tell everyone, to say those soppy things to him you only read in books, but I didn't dare.

Only last week he'd been looking to get blown by a bird and now he'd just moved in and was fucking me every night. I dare not lose this chance of happiness by turning him off with promises of undying love. I slid my body down his and took his hot throbbing cock straight in my mouth and deep down my throat causing myself to choke badly. Even so, I made myself continue in the hope of changing the subject and giving myself something else to think about. To no avail.

His hands pulled my head from his cock, and then moving under my shoulders pulled my body upwards, back where it had been before.

'And? What about us? How do you and I together fit in your scene?'

I sat up quickly. 'It's not a scene with us. It's more than that; you're more than that, so much more.'

Reaching behind me I grasped his hot hard cock and raising my body impaled myself quickly on that sign of his virility.

'And it's not just this either,' I gasped as my body adjusted to this welcome intrusion.

Maybe with such closer contact I could continue. I couldn't look at him; instead let my eyes fall on his chest where my fingers were drawing unseen circles through his dark chest hairs.

His hands grasped my wrists to stay their movement, 'Don't mess me around boy.'

I still couldn't look him in the face. 'With you it's different. All you have to do is slap me, spit on me, even piss on me, just abuse me and I start separating even before I feel any pain. I don't seem to float away anymore though, not when you're there. I merge with you somehow, seem to see through your eyes, I can feel your enjoyment; I want you to hurt me, need you to hurt me harder so we can enjoy it more. I know it's crazy but that's what happens. Even when you came back during the week I felt a change inside myself whenever you looked at me and each time you fucked me I took something from you that I can only return by sharing my pain and seeing your enjoyment.'

While I'd been talking his fingers had moved of their own accord it seemed, to my nipples where they, at any rate, were enjoying pinching and twisting while his cock was trying its very best to force a way deeper inside my backside. That part of him at any rate was still interested.

He just lay there for quite a while, his groin thrusting from time to time and his fingers turning my nipples into beds of burning pain. Finally I just had to grab hold of his wrists myself and place his hands behind his head bringing my face in line with his own but I still couldn't look him in the face.

'You do know I'm gay really?'

His words hit me harder than any belt across the ass and my head flicked up to look down on him. His deep eyes were wide open, looking up at me without any sense of dissimilation.

'I've always known it, deep down. Just never found the right man to admit it with before. Probably why I tend to hire gay mechanics for my shop.'

He was so open now, so straightforward, as if admitting to being gay was now the most normal thing in the world.

If those remarks had knocked me back, what he said next blew me away.

'The problem is,' he continued, 'I don't want to go round hurting people so how come I enjoy hurting the man I love?'

That did it! I yelled, I think, just before slamming my mouth down on his and trying my best to swallow his tongue and replace it with my own. His cock popped from my ass when I lay over him, my arms holding his wrists still behind his head and my legs attempting to wind tightly round his own, there was no way he would escape now. I know he'd said he loved me last night but thought that was sex talking, but now I could see the truth, and the pain, behind his words.

I could hear myself talking gibberish as my mouth moved back and forth, kissing his beautiful eyes, nibbling his ear lobes, his chin, back to his mouth every time he tried to get a word in.

'I love you too. I didn't dare say it in case you ran away. I love all of you, every little bit of you. I couldn't go on without you. Do you really love me?'

I ran down in the end of course, one can only carry on like that for so long. I didn't let him go though; just lay my head on his breast listening to his heart beating. His hands that I had released were playing with my hair.

'I knew something happened the moment I saw your face while that man was laying a belt across your naked body. But I shouldn't get off on hurting you.'

'Why on earth not?' I asked him. 'You enjoyed it, whipping me, fucking me in the sling last night and watching the candles drip on my body didn't you?'

'Shit yes.'

'Then its time you remembered who's supposed to be in charge here and make proper use of your boy hadn't you.'

A sudden twist and flip had me flat on my stomach with Karl sitting on my shoulders attacking the cheeks of my backside unmercifully with his hands, one after the other, then both together.

'Yes. It's about time I showed you who's boss around here boy.'

He soon had me jerking around under him, tears running down my face to soak unnoticed into the grass.

'Stop it, no more, please stop.' I didn't care who might hear me.

Karl shifted his body slightly, 'Do you really want me to stop. Your cheeks are only pink so far.'

'No Sir. Of course you shouldn't stop until you want to.'

He resumed his attack, this time with a belt he must have picked up from the side. I took little attention when he moved to kneel beside me and changed the direction of his blows to encompass my shoulders and back, then returning to my ass cheeks, I was too busy attempting to claw my way into the grass, my arms and legs spread-eagled without needing restraint, my head turning from side to side my face covered in tears and grass cuttings and dirt, my body writhing and jumping to the force of his blows, I could somehow see the heat rising from my inflamed rear.

I saw him drop the belt and kneel between my wide-open thighs to hold his open palms above my cheeks and pull back with a start, almost as if burnt by them. Then firmly using a couple of fingers from each hand to probe, and then penetrate my hole, to force an entry and twist and pull and press at the tender insides.

I yelled, well someone did. I saw and heard them but it didn't concern me. All that concerned me was the pain, the glorious pain saturating my body inside and out, permeating the surrounding area, the knowledge of a massive hot solid throbbing cock poised above those hot red cheeks.

'Go on! Take me Karl! Fuck my, fuck your boy, for Gods sake do me now!'

He did!

No sooner were his fingers pulled from my open ass his ramrod of a cock replaced them, plunging straight in to skewer my body to the ground before the lips of my hole had any chance of closing. As if that were not enough I felt every hair of his body sting against my inflamed skin when he wrapped his legs over mine and his arms under my chest bringing his fingers to my mouth.

'Suck on these boy, help keep your noise down.'

I'd not been aware my body was yelling and crying out until sucking gratefully on those fingers just removed from my asshole reduced it to a series of moans and groans allowing the external sounds to intrude. I could hear the grass rustling around us now, somewhere crickets chirping and birds settling in the branches overhead for the night quite oblivious to our actions, but above all Karl's voice murmuring in my ear.

Turning my head to one side but still sucking on his fingers it shocked me to see tears slowly running down his cheeks again as he looked at me.

'That hurt didn't it?'

There was no need to answer; I just bit his fingers lightly.

'I felt every blow,' he continued. 'This hurts as well,' he squeezed my body tighter, the heat from my sore back and cheeks slowly transferring to his chest and groin, I nipped his fingers again. 'And this?'

Karl flexed his cock buried so deeply inside me. I could feel every hot solid throbbing inch of him and it was true, each time either of us flinched or I clenched my ass cheeks his cock would flick and hit another sensitive section of my insides. This time I opened my mouth to reply.

'Yes Thank you Sir,' I managed to splutter round his fingers.

'Why thank me?' he came back with a grin, 'Wait to I fuck you, you may change your mind.'

'Then fuck me. Please! Please! Fuck me now!' I knew he was close and didn't think I could hold out much longer myself.

Karl moved his hands, one under my chest to close round a sore engorged nipple and as I gasped and writhed against that the other somehow managed to close tightly round the base of my cock squeezing my balls. I opened my mouth to yell and his lips clashed with mine so I screamed down his throat when he squeezed and twisted tighter, my body jerked and writhed, my ass clenched and he shot stream after stream of boiling Karl man juice inside me. He was yelling back with joy and I was swallowing it, his release down my throat while my ass continued to milk his connection.

Everywhere hurt. My back and ass, my face and head, my whole body was being knocked against the ground and shaken around, I needed to breathe, I needed --- I came. The harder he squeezed and pulled on my balls the more I came, over and over and over again. It flooded out of me, that glorious finale this had all been working to.

I never even felt him pull out, was only half aware when Karl brought his hand to my lips and I reabsorbed some of the protein I'd just been ejaculating, when he stood over me and unleashed a full bladder over my abused body before laying back down beside me, turning my weary head to face his.

There were still tear tracks down his cheeks; I stuck out my tongue to lick them.

'Why?' I asked.

'I felt it, felt something, felt you. I felt your pain but couldn't stop; I knew you wanted more even when you screamed for me to stop. I felt my cock rape your ass and knew you wanted it.'

'Why cry then?' I asked him. 'It was good wasn't it?'

'Oh yes! The best, the best ever. Now I know, know we connected somehow, I want more.'

'Oh we will. I'm sure you will think of lots of ways to enjoy me,' I told him. 'And we can connect without sex now, that I can feel, deep inside me. Anyway, I'll need time to recover before you let that out again. I'll need to sleep on my stomach again tonight anyway.'

'That's OK,' Karl smirked, 'You'll be in the right position to take care of my morning wood then.'

And of course he made sure I was, for that morning wood and many, many, more.

– MASTER –

A SHORT HOMOEROTIC S&M STORY

He waited, apprehensively.

Finally he would meet his possible future face to face after so many weeks of emails, chats and just a few one-way short web cam contacts. He still had no idea what his visitor really looked like, only had unsupported details to go on.

The front door was unlocked and he knelt in the middle of his hallway, virtually naked, head bowed, as instructed.

He waited, in trepidation.

Would he be acceptable? Would his visitor take one look at him from the door and walk away in disgust at a wasted journey, or possibly worse, use him briefly, painfully, as a sex toy and then throw the damaged goods to one side?

He waited, with some fear.

Would allowance be made for his inexperience, for his low pain threshold? Would this man be prepared, be willing, to take his time and build up slowly, or expect boy to suffer excessively right from the start?

He waited, had he gone too far?

His messages to the man had contained fantasies far in excess of anything boy could contemplate undertaking in real life, even allowing it had been agreed that his limits were to be extended. The little play he'd experienced while out cruising or as self-infliction would be, he knew, be nothing in comparison to what might happen this evening.

He waited, eagerly.

It was five minutes past the arranged time. Had he got everything ready as commanded? Large plastic sheet covered with an old towel on the floor. Flasks of boiling water for instant coffee and soft drinks in the fridge, his case of toys laid open for the mans inspection and use, a new bottle of poppers and a selection of DVD's including the short S&M films downloaded from the net the man wanted to see. Candles, extra trays of ice cubes in the freezer. Had he forgotten anything?

He waited, in anticipation

It was ten minutes past the arranged time. Was his body prepared as instructed? His bowels had been flushed out for the first time, he had rubber wrist and ankle restraints already fastened on his body, the neck collar lay to one side to be fitted by his visitor. A selection of luggage elastics and ropes lay to one side, ready to be attached from the restraints on his body to appropriate articles of furniture, His tightest cock ring was fitted behind his cock and balls, his shaved balls themselves were fitted with a separator strap ready to be stretched or squeezed. His only clothing was a short length of towel pulled between his thighs and tucked front and rear through a belt round his waist.

'I don't want to see your privates before I'm ready to abuse them,' he'd been told, 'but when I do I want quick access.

He waited, impatiently.

It was fifteen minutes past the arranged time. The boy started to panic. After all the arrangements, all the messages, had it all been a tease? Had the man changed his mind? He just couldn't go through this again, the effort it had taken him to overcome his terror of being placed, quite defenseless and unable to escape, at another's mercy, to have his body used for another's enjoyment without any recourse to flight.

He waited, despondently.

It was twenty minutes past the arranged time. The boy rose awkwardly from his position by the front door, his knee joints ached, and he couldn't stop his body from trembling. This wasn't from fear, this wasn't from relief, this was his mind reacting to the knowledge his body would not finally be receiving the punishment it so desperately had been crying out for.

He waited, in some discomfort.

Now twenty-fi minutes past the hour showed on his clock. His bladder was full as instructed and had now become painful. Where had he gone wrong? Had the whole thing been a fraud? Had his chatty emails caused the man to change his mind? Was it his fault?

He stopped waiting when the clock chimed the half hour.

Watched someone else's hands close the locks and then walk slowly from the hall to the living room and looked around. All those mails and chats, all those preparation, it all been a waste. His life would remain unfulfilled. He needed a toilet.

The doorbell!

He turned and half ran uncomfortably back down the hall, his ass cheek clenched against the pressure on his bladder, then slowed to a stop. It was thirty minutes past the arranged time, suppose this wasn't him? He could see his near naked body in the hall mirror; it could be anyone out there, even more than one person.

A fist hammered on the door.

He took a deep breath, slid back the bolts and then slowly opened the door, squinting his eyes against the setting sun whose rays shone almost directly through the open door causing the dust motes to sparkle as they drifted through the air. He had no eye though for the iridescence dance they made, neither for the glorious red sunset, no thought for anybody passing on the pavement, all eyes and thoughts concentrated on the man standing before him.

There had been no lies. He was probably in his thirties, six foot, thick short cut curly black hair, brilliant white teeth, clean shaven, a trim, well proportioned fit body, wearing a white polo shirt, dark blue shorts and white leather trainers. The only surprise he felt while looking into his visitors' deep eyes was that he'd never considered the color of his visitors skin. A deep dark mahogany, almost black, a skin so shiny, so smooth, emitting a slight hot aroma of sweet sweat and musk he immediately wanted to reach out and savor.

'Why was the door locked boy? Why aren't you in the proper position? Can't you understand simple instructions?'

These questions were accompanied by a couple of light slaps back and forth across boys face in full view of anybody who might be passing and looking through the still open doorway but he had no care about that.

He immediately sunk to his knees before his new god, his eyes streaming tears, his body heaving with emotion. What could he say? There was no excuse.

The man moved one leather trainer clad foot and pressed it against boy's crotch. That had been the arrangement; boy could only talk if his balls were being squashed. The pressure, light as it was, against his full bladder was excruciating.

'Why are you crying boy? I didn't hit you that hard.'

Boys' response was to grab the foot and press it harder against his privates, grinding it painfully against his balls and bloated bladder.

A hand grabbed hold of his hair, forcing him to look upwards. 'I asked, why are you crying?'

Boy knew he had to tell the truth.

'I thought you weren't coming Sir.'

'And now I'm here?'

Boy only had one possible answer for that as he stared back in elation.

'Master.'

———

– ABOUT THE AUTHOR –

ANTHONY THOMAS

Anthony is a frustrated mid aged submissive in the UK who discovered his S&M inclinations later on in life and never found the strength to submit sufficiently to really fly. My stories are, regrettably, pure fantasy and should be recognised as such, especially in respect of the abuse inflicted on my poor narrator's bodies. Also they tend to practice extremely unsafe sex and have never heard of condoms. Please don't try to emulate them; I want you to stay around to enjoy my efforts.

Cambridge, UK. April 2009

Author as a young man

www.ingramcontent.com/pod-product-compliance
Lightning Source LLC
Chambersburg PA
CBHW071210260626
47162CB00004B/1251